THE SLAYER CHRONICLES

THIRD STRIKE

▼

▸ HEATHER BREWER ◂

THE SLAYER CHRONICLES

THIRD STRIKE

DIAL BOOKS ·

An imprint of Penguin Group (USA) LLC

To Gwen Kelley, who's taught me to be strong
and who's shown me that good things come to those
who keep moving forward

▼   ▼   ▼

DIAL BOOKS
PUBLISHED BY THE PENGUIN GROUP
Penguin Group (USA) LLC, 375 Hudson Street, New York, New York 10014

USA I Canada I UK I Ireland I Australia I New Zealand I India I South Africa I China
penguin.com

A PENGUIN RANDOM HOUSE COMPANY

Copyright © 2014 by Heather Brewer

Library of Congress Cataloging-in-Publication Data
Brewer, Heather. • Third strike/Heather Brewer. • pages cm.—(The Slayer chronicles; 3)
Summary: Joss is given a mission to eradicate vampires in his home town of Santa
Carla, where he will need to protect his family, including cousin Henry, who still
carries a grudge. • ISBN 978-0-8037-3785-3 (hardcover) • [1. Vampires—Fiction. 2. Family
life—California—Fiction. 3. California—Fiction. 4. Horror stories.] I. Title.
PZ7.B75695Thi 2014   [Fic]—dc23   2013014215

Printed in the United States of America • 10 9 8 7 6 5 4 3 2 1
Designed by Jason Henry • Text set in Meridien

▶ ACKNOWLEDGMENTS ◀

Writing a book isn't easy. Writing a series is even less easy. And writing two series that coincide, like The Chronicles of Vladimir Tod and The Slayer Chronicles, is next to impossible. It's an effort that's required an incredible team of incredible people, and now that these stories are coming to a close, I want to send my heartfelt thanks to all of you for helping me move from the eighth grade, all the way to London and beyond, from the discovery of Elysia, to the oppressive shadows of the Slayer Society. Without you, this world might not have existed anywhere outside of my imagination. So thank you.

Michael Bourret—You are the best agent on the planet, and I am deeply indebted to you for all of the wonderful advice, guidance, and support that you've given me. You're a good friend, a great partner, and I wouldn't have come this far without you and all that you do. Here's to the future—may it be dark, stormy, and spooky, but only in all of the right ways.

Maureen Sullivan and Liz Waniewski—You were both such amazing editors. So patient, so brilliant. Thank you for helping me share Vlad and Joss with my Minions in the way that they deserved. I've learned so much from both of you, and send you nothing but love and gratitude.

All of the school and library, marketing and publicity folks at Penguin Young Readers—You got my books into the hands of my Minions. Without your thoughtful outreach and hard work, so many of the Minion Horde wouldn't have found themselves in Vlad or Joss. I appreciate all that you've done, and send you chocolate chip cookies . . . and maybe a steaming mug or two of AB negative.

The amazing art team at PYR and the incomparable Christian Fuenfhausen—You gifted me with the coolest covers and most FANGtastic mascot on the planet. Thank you, thank you, thank you. I owe you big-time.

Paul, Jacob, and Alexandria Brewer—Life is a lot like a book series. Some lives are like two book series that coincide. There are a ton of twists and turns, and sometimes it feels like the plot points will never come together just right. But if you stay true to those core characters, if you believe in the central story, you'll find your way through. The three of you—the four of us—always help me find my way through anything that I face. I have existed in the darkness and in the light, but no matter where I have been or how I have felt at the time, you've always been there for me. You are all that matters in my world. And I am blessed to have you. Thank you for being my everything, and for helping me to move forward with my dreams.

Last, but never least, my Minion Horde—We've come a long way, Minions. You've trusted me and followed me to Elysia and back, and for that, I am immeasurably grateful. But I'm afraid I must ask you to follow me further, into unexplored territory now. And trust me once again.

You see, when I began writing The Chronicles of Vladimir Tod, I set out to reach a goal. I wanted to feel better about having been bullied in school, about feeling like such a freak in a world of so-called "normal" people. It seemed like an impossible thing to do, but I accomplished that goal. I wrote great books about a twisted vampire world—books that led me to another world, a world of Slayers and stakes and secrets. I discovered new things about myself, and I hope that you did as well. Because once those stories were printed on pages and glued into a cover, they became *your* stories. It became *your* world to explore and enjoy. Since that time, so many of you have created amazing fanfic tales about the characters that I created. And I love that. Please keep going. Because through you, Vlad and Joss live on into eternity. Through you, Henry keeps crackin' jokes at inappropriate times and Snow keeps being strong. Through you, Eddie Poe keeps being hungry for power, and Cecile keeps Joss's nights interesting. These books, this world, will never cease to exist. Because of you, Minions. Because of you.

But these are not the only stories I have to share with you. So take my hand, Minions. Go on, crowd in and squeeze my hand as hard as you need to. Because we're moving into a place where we haven't been before, a world beyond Vladimir Tod and Joss McMillan. But I'm here for you and always will be. Let's move forward together.

CONTENTS

▼ ▼ ▼

THE
SLAYER
CHRONICLES

THIRD
STRIKE

▼

PROLOGUE

Em carefully lifted the teapot from its place on the doily and poured the steaming blood into two ornate china cups. The color of the burgundy blood against the white of the china was bold and interesting, Em noted. Not like the color of blood soaked into a rug or spattered against the curtains. Perhaps it was the purity of both things, blood and china, she thought, that appealed to her in such a comforting way.

One cup had been placed in front of Em, and the other in front of her guest, who sat in the shadowed quiet of Em's parlor. Em offered her guest some sugar, but she politely declined. Em plopped three cubes into her cup, marveling at the crystallized sugar cubes as they melted away into the blood, and sat back with a sigh, content to blow the steam from her cup of AB negative—something an old friend had once described to her as the champagne of blood types.

"How exactly will you arrange for him to be alone?" The girl's words were softly spoken, and Em couldn't help but wonder whether or not she was up to the task. After all, it wasn't as if this boy, this Slayer called Joss McMillan, were someone easily disregarded. He was skilled. A dangerous quality for any human with a blood thirst for vampires. He had to be dealt with, and quickly. Em just hoped that she wasn't choosing poorly by sending this girl to do him in. Though her advantage was obvious, she was still young.

Very young, in comparison to her youthful-looking host.

Em sipped from her cup, and as she returned it to its saucer on the table, she dabbed at her lips with a napkin before placing the napkin in her lap. Not many were subjected to this old-world side of Em—the lady-like grace and appreciation of finer things. Not many often saw beyond her youthful appearance of wild colored hair and gothic-style clothing. Few had ever been invited into her parlor, but here she was, with this girl, debating whether or not the girl had what it takes to face an enemy of skill. She was very new to vampire life, as it were. Young, naive, and certainly not well trained. Em wondered if she should have just killed Joss herself, but the thought passed quickly through her mind before it disappeared once again. No. This was the right killer for Joss—the girl had a reluctant hunger inside of her to take the boy's life. And the boy clearly had a reluctance in him to face her. Hunting him down herself was a recipe for disaster, in Em's eyes. Em didn't hunt down the majority of those who have wronged her. She had people for that. People like this promising new protégée. "Everything's been arranged. Have you been in recent contact with your drudge?"

The girl picked up her cup at last and took a healthy drink, wincing as she burned her tongue. She nodded as she bit into a thin wafer cookie in an effort to soothe her mouth. Through a mouthful of cookie, she said, "I have. My drudge stands at the ready to assist me."

Em wrinkled her nose at the girl's lack of manners. Truth be told, she'd killed kings and queens for less. But she liked this girl, this newborn vampire, for reasons that she could not yet identify. And so she let the girl live. For now, anyway. "I trust you know what will happen to you both if you fail to take the young Slayer's life?"

Her hands strangely steady, her voice oddly confident, the girl looked at Em and said with a tone that conveyed that she was well aware of what was at stake here, "If I don't kill Joss, you'll kill us both."

"Wrong." Em's lips curled into a cruel, sadistic smile. "If you fail in your task, I won't just kill you both. I'll obliterate your remains and lick your blood from my walls."

There was a pause—a distinct one—before the girl responded. But when she did, her voice sounded just as confident, just as driven as Em had been hoping it would. She returned her cup to its saucer and reached for another cookie. As the sweet treat reached her lips, she smiled in a way that mirrored Em. "Don't worry. I'm looking forward to taking Joss's life away. He deserves it for what he did to me."

Em released a breath in a soft sigh, settling back in her chair, satisfied. Her eyes moved casually over the walls of her suite. "That's good to hear, young one. Because I rather do like this wallpaper. It would be a shame to have to replace it."

▸ 1 ◂

THE RETURN OF THE
INVISIBLE BOY

Joss took a deep breath and reached for his bedroom doorknob once again. He couldn't hide upstairs all day, and if his dad found out that he was
standing in his room when there was entertaining to
do, he'd ground Joss on the spot. But Joss had needed
just a few minutes to escape the noise and the laughter
and the warm bodies that hosting a family reunion at
their home had created. He'd needed just a moment
to himself, without questions about his school and
friends he didn't have, and the occasional sympathetic
gleam in someone's eyes whenever anyone brought
up the word "sister" or the name "Cecile." What Joss

really needed was some time to put on his happy face, his normal teenager mask, when he was anything but. And it's not like he was the only one in his immediate family who was pretending.

"Joss! Get your butt outside. Now!" His dad was calling from outside, but he might as well have been standing right next to Joss, his voice was so loud, so full of a tension that had grown by leaps and bounds in the past few years. What would Joss give to ease that tension?

Just about anything.

Ever since relatives had begun pouring into their home this morning, his dad had been wearing a plastic smile and referring to Joss as "son"—always with a hearty slap on the back, like they were buddies or something. But his plastic smile, his plastic, cheery voice had slipped just then, and Joss wondered if anyone else had noticed.

Joss's mom wore a smile as well, but only when someone else—someone who hadn't been subjected to the downfall of their immediate family—was looking. But Joss could still see the shadows lurking in her eyes. He could feel the pain wafting off of her in a way that all of their extended family couldn't—or wouldn't—in the spirit of keeping this gathering relatively pleasant. It was as if the three of them were merely players putting on an act for the rest of the world to see. A strange play called *Normal Family*, and Joss had the starring role.

It was false, this image, but for whatever reason they all felt the need to take part in it, to fool the world, even though Joss was relatively certain that they weren't fooling anyone. But everyone pretended—even their audience. It was like clapping after the failed performance of a sad troupe of clowns. People felt bad for them. People pitied them. But no one truly believed them.

Readying himself, Joss donned his fake, polite smile and opened the door to the hall, leaving backstage behind. It was time for Act Two.

The moment the door was opened, the sounds of family and joyous laughter filled his ears. Joss moved along the short hallway and down the narrow stairs into the kitchen, where he exchanged smiles with Aunt Matilda before she whisked a big bowl of some kind of creamy dip off the counter and into the living room. Joss's mom followed her with an armload of bags of chips, but as she did, she called over her shoulder, "Joss, please help Henry with those vegetables."

Sitting at the counter on a bar stool, his shoulders hunched, looking miserable and angry and on the verge of an explosive outburst, was Henry. A voice from their shared past whispered through Joss's memory when he saw his cousin. *"We'll always be brothers."*

Even though there were only a few feet of space between the two cousins, it might as well have been a mile-wide chasm. And Joss wasn't certain that the chasm could ever be healed. It was a wound in their shared world. One he'd caused. One that Henry was keeping open. Maybe things would never get back to what they had been before the incident with Vlad. With the stake. With the Society.

On the counter in front of Henry sat a cutting board, a paring knife, a tray half full of sliced vegetables, and a bowl of whole carrots, celery, broccoli, and cauliflower. Joss approached slowly, the way one might approach an animal in the woods. "Need some help?"

Without warning, Henry stabbed the tip of the knife into the cutting board, so that the knife stood on end. It wavered a tiny bit before stopping, its blade catching the light in a way that made it shine. He met Joss's eyes, his jaw tight, his every muscle looking wound up like a spring that was about to break. "Why don't you do it? You're the one who's so good at stabbing things. Y'know . . . like people."

At first, Joss didn't know what to say or do. He hadn't seen Henry since he'd staked the vampire Vladimir Tod in Bathory, and Henry clearly hadn't forgiven him for having done so, or come to understand Joss's reasons. Vlad had been Joss's friend—or so Joss had thought. But Vlad was also a vampire. And killing vampires was Joss's job. But more than that, it was his mission in life to defend mankind . . . of which his cousin Henry was a part. But Henry refused to understand that. "Are you ever going to let that go?"

Henry stood and moved past him, knocking his shoulder into Joss's. As he did, he said, "No. So that should be the last time you bother to ask."

Joss didn't respond or even look after Henry as he left the room. He merely stood there, stunned at how much his life had changed in just a few short years, and not knowing whether it would ever again resemble anything at all what it used to be, or if the fiction that it had become would go on forever.

After a few quiet minutes finishing the vegetable tray, Joss cleaned up and carried the tray into the living room, where the majority of his relatives were gathered. Some of the men were outside, emptying brown bottles with enthusiastic grins and commenting on the meat as Joss's dad flipped it over on the grill. But one man in particular was still indoors, and it made Joss's smile switch from false to genuine the moment he saw him. Uncle Mike—or Big Mike, as everyone called him—looped his arm around Joss's head, tugging him closer, almost knocking the tray from his hand. Then he rubbed his knuckles into Joss's hair before letting him go. "Hey, Jossie Boy, what are you up to?"

Joss couldn't help but grin. His uncle Mike just had a welcoming, happy air about him, like a lighthouse to a lost crew. After setting the tray on the coffee table next to the dip, Joss turned back to his uncle and beamed. "Not much. I saw Henry in the kitchen. He seemed . . . upset."

He wasn't sure why he'd brought it up exactly. There was nothing that anyone, not even Big Mike, could do to mend what was broken between Joss and his cousin. Because the truth was that Joss had staked Vlad, intending to kill him, and Henry would never forgive him for that. But what Henry didn't know was that a small whisper of doubt had entered Joss's mind just before the stake had made contact with Vlad's skin, and Joss had moved the weapon slightly to the left on purpose, knowing that Vlad would likely survive.

Because Joss wasn't sure how he felt about Vlad, exactly. How he felt about Dorian. How he felt about vampires in general. He was confused. But Henry wouldn't understand that either.

Big Mike ruffled Joss's hair with his enormous hand. "Don't you let Henry's foul mood get you down, Jossie Boy. That boy's been moody for months now. I think it's girl troubles, myself, but your Aunt Matilda thinks he and his buddy Vlad—you remember Vlad—are having issues. He'll get through it. Just don't you mind him until he does."

He wished he could believe his uncle, but he couldn't. Because Joss knew very well that Henry's issue wasn't with some random girl or his best friend—it was with Joss, and Henry had already made up his mind about him.

"Joss, would you please take these steaks out to your dad?" Without awaiting an answer, his mom handed him a plate of thick, red, raw meat.

With a shrug at Uncle Mike—because Joss didn't really have any idea how to respond to him about Henry—Joss made his way through the crowd and out the side door. He was glad to see so many family members outside, because it would make speaking to his dad a lot easier. Speaking through their masks was so much more pleasant than interacting the way that they did whenever no one else was around. "Hey, Dad. Mom sent these out for you."

His dad smiled his fake smile and took the plate, offering Joss a semi-grateful nod. Then a hand fell on Joss's shoulder. When Joss turned his head, resisting his Slayer instincts to flip the unseen person over his shoulder and pin them on the ground, he realized that it was his cousin Greg, Henry's older brother. Greg was looking tan and fit, as usual, dressed in tan cargo shorts and a black tank top. "Hey, Joss! How ya doin', man? Listen, do you mind if we talk?"

Before Joss could utter a word, Greg was steering

him away from the grill, and away from all the people. Joss didn't feel alarmed at all, just relieved to not be onstage for the moment, as he and Greg crossed the lawn to the forest's edge that bordered the property. Just at that edge, Greg stopped and gave him a look that said that he was worried. "What's going on with you and Henry, kid?"

Joss swallowed hard and shrugged, trying desperately to put his mask back on so that his cousin wouldn't see how upset the whole situation really made him. But Greg saw the scramble and tossed that metaphorical mask on the ground with a sigh. "Joss, it's clear you two are fighting. But about what? I can't help you if you don't tell me what's going on. You guys used to be so close, and then suddenly every time someone at my house says your name, Henry's eyeballs catch on fire. What's up?"

At least Joss knew that he wasn't misinterpreting Henry's fury toward him. He shrugged one shoulder in response, but when Greg crossed his arms in front of his chest, Joss knew that he wasn't about to accept aloofness for an answer. He raked his hair back from his forehead with an exasperated sigh. "I don't know, Greg. I guess . . . I guess Henry just doesn't like me anymore."

He wasn't exactly certain what Greg's response to that might be, but he did know that he hadn't been expecting what Greg said next.

"Well, that's crap." Not so much as a smile on his lips. Not even the hint of one.

Joss blinked. "What?"

Greg shook his head. "*Of course* he likes you. He's your cousin. He's your friend. But it seems like he's worried about you. Any idea why that might be?"

There were a million reasons that Henry should be worried about Joss. The danger of vampires. The risky missions. The price that Dorian had warned him had been placed on his head by Em. But Joss was fairly certain that Henry wasn't worried at all. He was pretty convinced that Henry was angry. Because Joss had staked Vlad. And Henry's mind had been clouded when he was turned into Vlad's human slave.

Joss met his cousin's gaze. "Greg, I don't think he's worried about me, but I am worried about him. This Vlad kid—"

"Hold up. Vlad? You mean the kid who was your best pal for much of the last school year? The kid who's been like a second little brother to me since day one? That Vlad?"

Joss paused. He didn't want to get Greg worked up or ticked off at him, too. So instead, he chose more gentle words. "You don't have to get defensive. I just . . . Vlad's not who you think he is, that's all. I'm not saying he's a bad guy or anything, I'm just saying . . ."

What was he saying? Even he wasn't sure. What he really wanted to do was to grab Greg by the shirt collar and scream into his face, "He's a vampire, okay? Vladimir Tod is a dangerous creature that will bite you and suck the lifeblood from your veins!" But he didn't. He remained calm. Even though it was killing him to do so.

Greg uncrossed his arms at last and sighed. "Then what are you saying, Joss? Because if you know something that I don't, if Vlad is getting mixed up in some bad stuff, I need to know. I can't let my brother follow him down a bad path."

Or a dark one, thought Joss. Or an alley. Or anywhere that they might be alone, without witnesses to the horrors that Vlad was capable of. But he didn't put voice to any of those thoughts. Instead, he said, "I'm just trying to help Henry see that maybe Vlad isn't as good as he thinks he is, that's all."

"That's all?" Greg's posture relaxed, but he went back to shaking his head. "No wonder his eyes catch on fire like that. You've gotta be careful, Joss. Vlad's been as close to Henry as a friend can get since they were kids. You've really gotta get a grip on your jealousy. Vlad is Henry's friend, but you're family."

Jealous? Is that what Greg thought? Joss wasn't jealous of Vlad. He was merely trying to protect his cousin. But how could he make Greg understand any of that without exposing the existence of vampires and the Slayer Society? "That's not what I—"

"Joss. A word, if you please."

Joss turned his head at the familiar voice. A strange tension entered his body the moment his eyes met with that of the speaker's. "Uncle Abraham. When did you get h—?"

"A word." Abraham's eyes narrowed. In stark contrast to what Greg was wearing, Abraham donned his usual slacks, shirt, and vest. Over it, he wore a tweed jacket with patches on the elbows; he was looking very much like his cover story, a successful university professor. "If you don't mind, Greg."

"No problem, Uncle Abraham." Greg looked back to Joss before walking away to rejoin the men by the grill. "Just remember what I said, kid. Jealousy isn't healthy."

Joss couldn't say anything to that. He wasn't jealous. He was just trying to do a very important, very secret job.

"Who are you jealous of, nephew? Greg? Henry? Either would be an apt choice. Both are physically adept, confident young men." He cast Joss a sidelong glance. "Either would make a fine Slayer."

Joss wouldn't allow himself to feel any of the barbs that his uncle might throw at him. He knew very well that his uncle hadn't exactly been accepting of the notion that Joss was the next Slayer in his family line. "I assume you're not just here for the barbecue."

The corner of Abraham's mouth lifted in a small, knowing smile. "I have your next assignment."

Relief flooded over Joss. His next assignment. That meant that he'd be leaving Santa Carla for the summer. It meant he'd be spending time with his Slayer family, the few people on this planet who could actually understand the enormous pressures and responsibility that Joss was facing on a regular basis. It meant that he was going home. For the summer, at least.

From inside his sports coat, Abraham pulled a small parchment envelope bearing the red wax seal of the Slayer Society. As he handed it to Joss, he said, "This mission will require stealth in a way that you've not yet achieved, nephew. You'll have to decide exactly how to remain hidden in this scenario, and it won't be easy for you, I'm afraid."

"Is it ever?" The words passed over his lips in a whisper before he'd had a chance to truly examine how they might sound to his uncle, his mentor. Fortunately, Abraham either hadn't heard them, or ignored them completely.

"You're on your own this time, Slayer. Your team has assignments in other cities, myself included. This task falls to you and you alone, by the bequeath of the

Society. Only Paty will remain behind with you, but strictly to act as liaison between you and the Society elders. She cannot help you in your task."

Joss furrowed his brow and turned the envelope over in his hands curiously. He rubbed his thumb along the wax seal and pondered, "What's my assignment, exactly?"

"Intel has shown that there are vampires running wild in a certain small town, picking off human townsfolk whenever the mood takes them. You need to track down the creatures and stop as many of them as you possibly can before a cleansing of the town becomes necessary."

A cleansing. The Slayer Society would sweep through the town, killing everyone—both vampire and human alike—wiping the slate clean. It had been done before, but not for a hundred years. Joss hoped that it would never be done again.

"Where am I going?"

"Nowhere."

Joss snapped his eyes to Abraham's.

Abraham cracked a smile, but Joss was damn certain that it wasn't a reflection of inner peace or joy. It was sadistic, that line in his mouth. It was cruel. The way that Abraham had been cruel. The way that Abraham was still cruel.

Then, as if to erase all doubts as to what he was saying, Abraham said, "The town of which I speak is the one in which you currently reside."

Joss's chest suddenly felt empty, hollowed out by the realization of what it would mean if he failed. His family was here. His parents. He swallowed hard, the name of the town escaping his lips in a disbelieving breath. "Santa Carla?"

Abraham tipped the brim of the brown fedora he was wearing in Joss's direction and smiled before turning to walk away. Over his shoulder, he confirmed Joss's query with a matter-of-fact tone and an almost singsong voice that grated on Joss's every last nerve. "Santa Carla. You'd think that with your training and keen eye, you might have noticed."

But Joss hadn't noticed. He hadn't noticed anything that suggested that vampires had infested the town in which he lived. Was he losing his touch? Or had he never really had one in the first place?

As his uncle walked away, Joss watched him, clutching the envelope in his hands, so tight between his fingers that he was amazed that the pages didn't crumble. Uncle Abraham joined the men who were still standing around the grill, even though Joss's dad had closed the lid and just begun to carry the plate of cooked food back into the house. Abraham smiled at them and they smiled back, sweeping him easily into their casual conversation. Joss realized then that while he and his parents were sad clowns, a pitiful act on a stage of sorrow, his uncle was a master of disguise. No one saw him for the Slayer that he was, or for the gifted liar that he had to be. Joss was torn between wanting to be like his uncle and hoping that he never became like him in any way.

Shock held Joss to that very spot—shock that his family was at risk. If he failed in his mission, they would die. It was as simple as that. Not to mention what it meant for Joss to face down multiple vampires on the loose—ones who'd decided that they were free to feed on the innocent people of Santa Carla at will, without repercussion. He didn't know if he was capable of taking the vampires out all by himself, without the aid of his skilled team members. He only knew that he was scared and worried for his family. He couldn't have felt more relieved that his extended family would be leaving town the next morning. At least Greg, Aunt Matilda, Big Uncle Mike, and the others would be safe. At least Henry would be safe.

But his parents . . .

No. Joss would do anything to protect them from the ravenous hunger of mad vampires on the run and the cleansing intent of the Slayer Society. Anything.

But he had to do so in a way that his parents wouldn't notice him. Because if they did, Joss's whole world would come crashing down around him. He'd have too much explaining to do, and he had no idea how to even begin such a task. How could he hide his vampire hunting and killing efforts from his parents, when doing such a thing resulted in so much blood, so many scars?

Joss suddenly wished that he was invisible. A slight breeze rustled through the trees, brushing his hair from his eyes. And then—strangely . . . ironically—he remembered that once their family reunion was over and everyone else had gone home, his parents would go back to their sad selves. And he would once again be the Invisible Boy.

But this time, it would be on purpose.

· 2 ·

THE SUDDEN ONSET OF
BEING AMISH

No one on the planet could have been more relieved than Joss the next morning when the last few relatives had packed up their cars and said their good-byes. Except, maybe, for Henry, who had picked up his suitcase and practically sprinted toward the rental car's trunk. Joss hurried to follow, wondering all the while whether his and Henry's friendship would ever, could ever, be mended. Not likely. Not the way that Henry was acting.

Standing at the rear of the car were Joss's dad and Big Mike. Just as Henry began to lift his bag and set it inside the open trunk, Big Mike laid a big hand on his shoulder. "Hold on there a second, Henry."

With a confused look in his eyes, Henry set the bag on the ground beside the car. "What's going on?"

Big Mike and Joss's dad exchanged a look. Relief flooded through Joss's veins. At least he wasn't the one in trouble this time. And besides that, maybe there was a hint of justice in the fact that Henry had been a total jerk to him all weekend and now he was getting yelled at for something. Joss straightened his shoulders and watched Big Mike, waiting for whatever storm that was coming. As he stood there, he swore he smelled a hint of rain, but there were no clouds overhead. Just another sunny, bright day in Santa Carla.

"It seems to me that you've been a tad disrespectful to your cousin here all weekend. I don't like it. And I know your mother doesn't like it at all. You boys have always been close, so whatever this is that's brewing between you, you should have the decency to put it aside when the family gets together for something like this reunion." With every word that left Big Mike's lips, Henry's muscles tightened visibly. Big Mike kept his voice even, but his voice was big too, like him, so it wasn't exactly something that Henry could ignore. Joss watched, grateful that he wasn't on the receiving end of things. "Now I want you to apologize to Joss for the way you've behaved toward him all weekend."

Joss raised an expectant eyebrow at his cousin. He

hated to admit it, but he was really enjoying this. Even if Henry's apology only sprang into existence because he was told to do so, it was a start. Besides, Henry *had* been rude to him all weekend, even if, on some level, Joss believed that he just might have deserved it. Steam practically escaped from Henry's ears the moment their eyes met. His cousin had always had a temper—and it had always made Joss laugh to see Henry lose it over something—but now that temper was being directed at Joss, and it wasn't so funny anymore.

Henry darted a glare at Joss, as if he'd set this entire thing up. Then he glanced at Joss's dad before turning his attention back to Big Mike. "Dad, you don't understand."

Big Mike chuckled. The sound of it reminded Joss of thunder in the distance. "Oh, I understand better than you might think, son. Cousins fight. Brothers fight. And you two are gonna stick together and work this out before it becomes unfixable."

Stick together? That made it sound like . . . but no. Henry was going home. Home, where he would be safe from a potential cleansing. Joss swallowed hard before asking, "What do you mean, exactly?"

Big Mike looked from Henry to Joss and back again. "We've been talking, and it seems like what you boys both need is some extended time together so you can fix whatever's broken between you."

Joss's heart thumped hard inside his chest. So much for feeling justified in Henry receiving any kind of punishment for having been a jerk. Now Joss was being punished, too, and he wasn't certain that he fully understood why.

His dad spoke then, and Joss was shocked to hear his actual tone—not the hurt, angry tone of a man who'd lost his daughter, not the false tone of a man who was just fighting to keep it together in front of other people, but his actual voice. The real him. Hearing it sent goose bumps up Joss's spine. It was like listening to the whisperings of a long-forgotten ghost. "And maybe, through doing that, whatever's broken in Joss can be mended, too."

Joss locked surprised eyes with his dad then. He had no idea that his dad even had an inkling that Joss had been facing anything difficult at all. If only he knew what.

His dad nodded, furrowing his brow sympathetically. "Clearly you're going through some heady stuff, son. Maybe this will help."

Clearly. Which meant that his dad had noticed. Which meant that maybe Joss wasn't so great, after all, at hiding the Slayer side of his life. But it also meant that his dad had seen him, and was worried about him—two things that he'd been convinced would never happen again.

Henry's face and neck were turning red, as if all of the blood in his body had gathered there. He refused to make eye contact with anyone. "So . . . you're saying . . ."

Big Mike slapped Henry gently on the back with his meaty hand. "We're saying you can drop this bag in the guest room next to Joss's bedroom, and Joss will be happy to spend the next month with his favorite cousin."

Henry looked at his dad. Joss looked at his. And after a long silence, the boys looked at each other. Neither looked happy.

Without another word, Henry picked up his bag and started carrying it toward the house. But he didn't get very far before Big Mike said, "One more thing, son."

Henry stopped in his tracks and turned around. Joss could tell by his demeanor that it was taking every ounce of self-control for Henry not to scream at his dad. "What? There's more?"

"Your cell phone, Henry. If you two are going to connect, you need no distractions. Hand it over." Big Mike held out his palm and instantly a kind of panic filled Henry's eyes. Joss knew it was panic, because he was feeling it, too.

His dad said, "You too, Joss."

His cell phone? But how was he supposed to call in

for a cleanup or assistance? What if he got into serious trouble with the rogue vampires and he needed to call for help? If he didn't have his cell phone, he'd be in the dark out there. Completely alone with his sworn enemies. His heart raced at the thought.

With a curse under his breath that Big Mike seemed to purposefully ignore, Henry slapped his cell phone into his dad's palm and stomped off to the house, leaving Joss standing there trying to think of an excuse his dad would buy for why he needed to keep his phone.

"Joss. Now." His dad meant business, and try as he might, Joss couldn't think of a believable lie to tell him.

He pulled the phone from his pocket and handed it to his dad. The moment his fingers released it, Joss felt a foreboding fear sink into his every pore. He was on his own now. With no way to call for help. And how was he supposed to take care of the vampire problem when he had to babysit his cousin for the next month? And if he failed . . . what would happen to Henry?

He knew very well what would happen to Henry. Henry, like Joss's parents, would die.

Joss's mom and Aunt Matilda made their way from the house to the car then, chattering every step of the way. Behind them was Greg, who had his hands and arms full of luggage and Tupperware containers. As Greg placed everything in the trunk, the rest of the family exchanged hugs and handshakes. Joss moved through the entire scene in slow motion. He didn't feel present at all. It was more like a dream. A bad one. And all Joss wanted to do was to wake up—preferably somewhere his home life and family were very much kept separate from his job as a vampire Slayer.

As Henry's family's car moved down the driveway and then down the road, Joss watched it, wondering exactly how he was supposed to handle all of this . . . and whether or not he was up to the task.

· 3 ·

VISITING PATY

s Joss climbed the stairs to his room, two things
happened at the same time. One, Henry slammed
the door to the guest room, sealing himself
inside. And two, Joss's mom called after him, "Joss,
don't forget to take the trash out."

He paused on the stairs, his eyes locked on Henry's
closed door, and answered his mom as an afterthought.
"In a second. Be right down."

He didn't know if their dads' plan would work, or
if it were even possible to mend this friendship, this
relationship, in the span of just four weeks. But he
did know that he hoped that they could come out on

the other side friends, or, at the very least, alive. It was unlikely, though. He was pretty sure Henry wanted him dead—or at least on the verge and twitching—for what Joss had done to Vlad.

Steal a guy's best friend and he can forgive you. Stake a guy's best friend through the back and he'll hate you to your core for all eternity.

Joss moved the rest of the way up the stairs and slipped inside his bedroom, closing the door gently, quietly, behind him. The moment it was closed, he pulled the Slayer Society letter from his back pocket and broke the seal. His uncle had given him most of the details already, but protocol dictated that he read the letter as well, in case extra details were located within. He scanned the letter, noting that Paty was staying in a cabin not too far from where his family's house was located. Smart move on the Society's part. Wouldn't want Joss hoofing it all the way across town, just to report his findings and activities to his team. The letter said that Paty was holding documents and further details for him, so Joss made a plan to escape his house for a bit and go see her.

There had been no sign of Uncle Abraham since the family reunion broke up. He hadn't even said good-bye or wished Joss good luck at all. That fact bothered Joss more deeply than he would ever admit to. He wanted his uncle's approval—as a man, as a Slayer—

but he was beginning to wonder if he would ever truly be the recipient of it. Just when he'd thought they were making headway, Abraham stepped back again, taking his approval with him. Joss loved his uncle . . . but despised him at the same time. It was horrible, being torn in two like that. And he was ashamed to even admit those feelings to himself.

He moved to the head of his bed and dropped quietly to the floor, removing a loose floorboard beneath where he lay at night. Even as he slipped the letter inside, Joss told himself that he shouldn't be doing this, shouldn't be keeping anything at all that might expose the existence of the Slayer Society. He'd been taught to burn all letters until they were nothing but ash and memories, so that no human would ever know that there was a secret organization in existence, protecting them from bloodthirsty monsters. But he couldn't help it. His job was utterly thankless. Sometimes he felt so unappreciated, as if he might as well not be doing anything at all to combat vampires, for all the praise it brought him. So late at night, whenever he was feeling sad or angry or bitter or alone, as the moonlight filtered in through the curtains, Joss would pull out the letters from the Society and his journal and read the words that proved to him that he was doing the right thing. Because he was. Even if he sometimes questioned whether or not vampires were the evil creatures the Society made them out to be.

An image flashed in his mind. The face of a teenage boy. He had black hair that hung in his eyes. And fangs. His name was Vlad. And Joss didn't know how that image made him feel. Guilty, mostly. And sad. And a little alone. He should have felt pride—he knew that. But mostly, he just felt confused.

Shaking the image away, Joss returned the loose floorboard to its place and stood, running a hand over the back of his neck in thought. He had to get out of the house for a while to visit Paty, but he wasn't certain how to do so without his parents suggesting that he take Henry along with him wherever he was going. Then in an instant, he had it. It was easier to ask forgiveness than permission. And his parents would just have to deal.

As quietly as he could manage, Joss slipped out his door, along the hall, and down the stairs to the kitchen. He tied the garbage bag closed, lifted it from the can, and mumbled in his mom's direction, "Taking the garbage out."

He wasn't even sure that she'd heard him. It was as if the moment Aunt Matilda had left the premises, Joss's mom had retreated once again inside of her cocoon. The sorrowful glaze had returned to her eyes.

The mourning of Cecile had resumed. Joss's heart cracked further as he opened the back door. His family was broken, and he wasn't at all certain how to mend them.

He hadn't lied to his mom—he was taking the garbage out. It's just that he'd failed to mention that once he dropped the bag in the can beside the house, he was going to keep walking until he rendezvoused with a fellow Slayer. Because Joss had a job to do. And though he wished that he had time to sit with his mom and coax her from her cocoon, he didn't. People were dying, and it was up to Joss to save them. Because if he didn't, they would all be dead soon. Including his family.

Dropping the bag in the can, Joss moved around and away from the house as quickly and quietly as he was able to, not wanting to be seen by his dad, who would inevitably have chores for him to do. Luckily, no one and nothing stopped his escape, and before Joss knew it, he was walking down the road, the sun gently baking his shoulders through his T-shirt, the sound of chirping birds filling his ears. It was a pleasant day, despite the gloom of his mother that still seemed so present in the back of Joss's mind.

It didn't take him long to reach Paty's cabin, their temporary headquarters. And Joss could see why the Society had chosen it as a base of operations. No one would ever suspect that a skilled vampire Slayer, capable of taking life quickly and completely, would reside in a house like this. It was a small house, painted a bright white, with cheery, colorful flowers planted all around its base. The garden spread from the house to the wooden railway fence that surrounded its small, charming yard. The shutters were a deep blue, and beneath each of the small windows were flower boxes containing multicolored daisies. A brief thought swept through Joss's mind at the sight of them.

Cecile would have loved those flowers.

But as soon as the thought had appeared, it was gone again, swept away by the pleasant, unexpected breeze, and Joss's unwillingness to think about his sister in the light of day. He'd decided over the last few days of his school year that Cecile would own his nights. But his days . . . his days had to belong to him, or else he might lose his mind entirely.

The nightmares had gotten worse. Then stopped. Then returned with a vengeance. Joss didn't sleep much anymore. When he did, he was chased by a monstrous version of his younger sister—one with deep, tunnel eyes and a mouth full of razor-sharp teeth. He wasn't certain anymore whether the Cecile from his dreams was a manifestation of his guilt for having failed to save her young life, or if she was an embodiment of evil, hell-bent on taking Joss's life. He just knew that sleep wasn't something he enjoyed, and the only thing he couldn't avoid forever.

When he opened the small gate, it squeaked and then banged closed behind him as he approached the cottage. He only just raised his fist to knock on the door when it whipped open and hands dragged him inside, slamming him against the wall. The lights dimmed briefly, but then his vision returned to find Paty's eyes widening in shock. Apologies flew from her mouth as she released him and closed the door. "Joss! Oh no! I am so sorry. You just never know who's coming, and I really had no idea it was you. I'm all on edge from being assigned to stay here alone and . . ."

She sighed and looked at him then, a frown pulling the corners of her pretty mouth down. "Are you okay? I really am sorry."

Apart from his heart being shifted into overdrive, Joss was fine. He smiled at her. "Y'know, come this fall, that's no way to greet trick-or-treaters."

Paty smirked. "But it's summer, so I'm good, right?"

Joss looked around the room. It was a small, relatively open floor plan. Cozy. Nice. "So does that mean you don't have any candy?"

She groaned then and gave him a playful punch in the arm before returning to the kitchen, where she'd been stirring something steamy and delicious smelling on the stove. "You're starting to sound like Morgan."

Joss sat on a bar stool by the kitchen island that held the stove, taking in the yummy smells. Chili, maybe. Or some kind of spicy soup. Paty picked up the wooden spoon and stirred the concoction, causing Joss's stomach to rumble. "How is Morgan, anyway? I was hoping—"

"You were hoping to see the team again, right?" She glanced up at him in that mothering way that she had about her. "It sucks that you can't, Joss. But the Society . . . things are weird. Something's . . . something's going on."

He plucked a clean spoon from the counter and dipped it into the pot. As he blew the steam from his stolen bite, he said, "Mind being more specific?"

Paty shook her head and ladled him a small bowl of her cooking. As Joss placed the spoon in his mouth, he recognized it as chili. Only Paty could make chili like this—with banana peppers and jalapeños. So delicious, so spicy, that Joss knew he'd crave it for days. As he began working on emptying his bowl, Paty wiped her hands off on a towel and sighed. "Who knows? Not me, that's for sure. All I know is that I was told that if I value my position as a Slayer, I'll stay out of your assignment. I've been instructed to give you the initial intel, act as liaison between you and the Society, and that's it. Or else."

Joss raised a sharp eyebrow at her. "Or else what?"

"That's just it, Joss. I don't know." Shaking her head, she returned the lid to the pot before meeting his eyes once again. "Anyway, if you need anything, just call. Not that it'll do much good. But I can call in for backup, if needed, and we'll see what happens."

He picked up the bowl, slurping the last bits of chili from it, and set it back on the counter with a frown. "My dad took my cell phone."

Paty shrugged. "I can get you another."

"No, thanks. If I get caught with a new phone, my parents would just ask questions that I don't have answers to. Besides, if all you can do is act as a liaison, then what's the point of the cell phone? If I need you, I'll knock." The corner of his mouth rose in a smirk. "Try not to assault me next time, okay?"

"I'll try." She looked at him then, for what seemed like a long time, as if she hadn't seen him in years, even though it had been only about nine months since they'd left Manhattan. "You're getting taller. And cuter. Got a girlfriend yet?"

Immediately, his thoughts were filled with the memory of a pretty girl in pink that he'd met back in Bathory. Meredith. He didn't yet have a girlfriend, but if he could, he wished more than anything that it could be her.

His cheeks warmed in a blush—one that Joss hoped wasn't apparent. "No."

"Working on it?"

"Not really. I don't exactly have time for girls."

"Or sleep?" She gestured to the circles beneath his eyes.

Joss looked away, pushing the empty bowl from him rather abruptly. "I'd rather not talk about that."

The air changed then. It grew quiet and restless. Uncomfortable, when Joss had been enjoying the comfort of it so much just a moment before. At long last, Paty said, "Fair enough. There's a manila folder on the mantel. Inside is everything we know about the killings in Santa Carla."

Joss excused himself and wandered into the living room. As promised, lying on the mantel of the small fireplace was a thin manila folder. Inside were various files and notes regarding recent deaths in Santa Carla, but nothing stood out to Joss. Nothing screamed *vampire*. He leafed through the papers as he walked back into the kitchen, taking his seat at the counter. Frowning, he looked from the papers to Paty, who was now wiping down the counters with a moist cloth. "Most of these deaths just seem like accidents or natural causes."

"Of course they do. Vampires love keeping their murders secret. Easier to kill again if no one suspects you the first time." She shrugged as she cleaned, as if this were the most normal, casual conversation to be having. He wondered instantly what Paty's life was like when she wasn't tracking down vampires and killing them. It occurred to him that he had no idea, and had never asked. It wasn't something that any of the Slayers seemed open to discussing. But Joss was curious, nonetheless.

"So why does the Society think that vampires are responsible, exactly?"

"Isn't it just a tad bit strange that so many of these deaths feature severed arteries and that several victims were noted to have been severely anemic?" She crossed the room to him then and flipped through the pages, stopping to point to several notes. "These are the kinds of details you need to pay attention to, Joss. A good Slayer knows that. Learn that early on and you could be one of the best Slayers out there in just a few years."

A good Slayer. Meaning that Joss wasn't one? It reminded him too much of what Abraham had said on the day of the barbecue. Maybe he wasn't as good at his job as he'd thought.

"You have a point. Worth looking into, anyway." He closed the folder and tucked it under his arm before going back to the door. Time was still moving, and he had work to do. Work that would take him away from the stress of spending the summer with his family, with his cousin. "I'll interview the four most recent victims' families, see if I can come up with anything."

"Joss." Her voice was soft and wavering, as if tears might not be far behind. It was enough to give Joss pause, with his hand on the doorknob. Paty hurried over to him, drawing her arms up around herself protectively. Her eyes darted around the room, as if someone other than the two of them might be listening. "I want to tell you something. Something that could land me in some very hot water, if anyone knew that I said anything."

He'd never seen Paty so distracted, so . . . unsettled before. It was unnerving. "What is it, Paty?"

Her eyes shimmered slightly and when she spoke, it was in worried whispers. "I haven't just been sent here to help you communicate with the Society. I've been sent here to watch your every move. So don't make any stupid ones, okay?"

His grip on the doorknob tightened. Could the Society be listening now? Would they bug Paty's house? Was that something the Society did? Were they—he swallowed hard—something to fear? "What happens if I do?"

She shook her head. "I don't know. I just know that I'd be lying if I said that I wasn't at least a little bit scared for both of us."

As he opened the door and stepped outside, he cast her what he hoped was a comforting smile. "Don't worry, Paty. Everything will be okay. I'm sure of it."

When he stepped into the sun, he didn't feel its warmth. Only the prickle of worry and doubt that Paty's warnings had filled him with. And there was something else. Something gnawing at the center of his being with every step that he took.

Every inch of him knew that what he'd just said to Paty was a lie.

4

SUPERMAN

Joss sat at the small desk in his bedroom, hunched over the glowing screen of his laptop. Every light was off in his room, and he was doing his best to click as quietly as he could with the trackpad and type as silently as he was able on his keyboard, for fear that his dad would hear.

He was as surprised as anyone when his parents bought him a laptop for his last birthday, but not surprised at all that his dad had put so many restrictions on his use of it. Joss couldn't use it when they had company, or chores, or after lights-out. So pretty much, never. Unless, of course, he snuck some time in without his parents finding out. Which was exactly what he was doing. Plus, the Internet was a great substitute for sleep—which was something that he wouldn't want to avoid at all, if Cecile wasn't waiting for him inside his dreams with filthy claws for fingers and a hungry mouth. So his stolen time online served two purposes, really.

He didn't enjoy breaking the rules, but at times he was forced to—whether by his parents or by the Slayer Society. Sometimes it felt like someone besides Joss was always running his life, always telling him what to do, always dictating what direction he should move in or what he should be doing. It made his chest feel tight—so tight that it was difficult to breathe—if he really thought about how little control he actually had over his own life. And that asthmatic feeling turned to a crushing sensation whenever he pondered that it would never end—not when he graduated from high school, not when he graduated from college. His life would always be controlled by someone other than himself. The Society would make certain of that.

Joss squeezed his eyes closed and sat back in his chair, pinching the bridge of his nose for a moment. Just long enough to willingly forget about how his life was not his own. Just long enough to squash that driving need to be in control of his own destiny.

With a stretch and a deep sigh, he returned his

attention to the screen, hoping that his rule break-ing would at least prove fruitful. On the screen was a photograph of a man in his midforties, with black curly hair that stopped just short of his shirt's collar, and bright blue eyes. Above the photograph was the article's title: LOCAL MAN KILLED BY PACK OF COYOTES. Above that was the newspaper's title, the *Santa Carla Sunset Times*.

The article was short and fairly straightforward, and one of only a few mentions that Joss could find of the man's passing available online. It stated that Hay-worth Banning, age forty-seven, had simply wandered out of his family-owned ice-cream shop one day, pre-sumably to go for a stroll, and had been attacked by a small pack of coyotes on the edge of the woods nearby. Nothing at all about the article struck Joss as unusual. People went for walks all the time. Coyotes were dan-gerous creatures. So he still wasn't certain why the Society had marked this man's death as something to investigate further, with an eye toward vampire involvement. Apart from the fact that the man had apparently been deemed almost unrecognizable by the family members who came to identify the body. But wild animals did that, too.

Joss glanced up at his window, which now framed the rising sun. He'd been so immersed in the work he was doing that he hadn't even noticed the sun was on the verge of coming up. And now the sky was bright orange and yellow. A new day had begun.

It disturbed him that his mind had been so deep into his task that he hadn't noticed the sun creeping up on him. What if a vampire had chosen that moment to attack him? It might have succeeded in killing him, all because Joss's head was stuck in the World Wide Web.

Dragging his finger across the trackpad, Joss shut his computer down. He really needed to spend less time online.

Besides, according to his research, the ice-cream shop was about a twenty-minute walk from his house and would be open in about two hours. It was crazy that it opened so early, but this was a tourist town, and such things just were.

He closed his laptop and grabbed some clean clothes on his way out of his bedroom door. After a quick, hot shower to help him wake up, Joss spent a long time brushing his teeth and trying not to fall asleep while standing up. The lack of rest was catching up to him. Catnaps were about all that he could manage without being tormented by Cecile and the nightmarish images that appeared inside his sleeping mind, but they weren't enough to make him feel truly rested. After he slipped into clean boxers, jeans, and a T-shirt, he rinsed his mouth, dropped his dirty clothes in the hamper, and hung the wet towel on the towel bar. Then, as quietly as he could, Joss descended the stairs and readied the coffeepot. Mornings like this called for caffeine. A lot of it.

There were many stark differences between Henry's house and his own, but a big one was morning. In Henry's house, Joss would stumble down the stairs to a cozy kitchen in the morning, where he was greeted by Aunt Matilda's cheery smile. The smell of bacon and eggs would tantalize his senses as he grabbed a seat at the table. Over a cup of steaming coffee and the morning paper, Big Mike would ask if he had any plans for the day. Then, as Joss shoveled food into his mouth, Aunt Matilda would insist that all plans waited until the boys had washed and dried the breakfast dishes and put them all away. And Joss was happy to do it. He was happy to have that familial obligation, the way he didn't really have it at home.

Since Cecile's passing, the kitchen at Joss's house was cool and lonely in the morning. If Joss wanted breakfast, he had better cook it himself, and it had better be Pop-Tarts. On occasion, his mom would already be sipping hot coffee when he made his way down the stairs, but she rarely greeted him, lost in her own world. His dad was never in the kitchen. There was no morning paper to read. Morning was a lonely time.

His parents didn't like him drinking coffee, but Joss

was sly. He grabbed a red mug from the corner cabinet that read "Keep Calm and Carry On" and turned it over in his hands. It was chipped slightly, evidence that this mug was his mom's favorite. He wondered how she was doing at that whole "carry on" thing, or if she could see the irony of a woman who was so frazzled, so broken, using a mug instructing her to do the very opposite. After pouring it full of hot coffee, he moved into the living room, where his mom was just sitting, and handed it to her. "Morning, Mom. Here's your coffee. Black, right?"

She nodded a thank you and blew the steam from her mug's contents. No smile. No cheery banter. Just a nod. But Joss would take it. Even though he was tempted to ask her if she was carrying on okay, he didn't ask because he already knew the answer. No. She wasn't okay. She wasn't carrying on very well at all.

He moved back into the kitchen and grabbed a second mug from the cupboard. This one read NOT ALL SUPERHEROES WEAR CAPES. Never a truer statement ever printed on a mug, he thought. He was like that— all the Slayers were. Superheroes with stakes instead of capes. He held it in his hand for a good long time before setting it on the counter and pouring himself half a mug of wake-up juice. After adding more cream and sugar than he'd ever seen either of his parents use, he gulped the sweet concoction down, rinsed out his mug, and glanced at the clock. According to their website, it was only about an hour until the ice-cream parlor opened—though Joss had no idea what kind of person would want ice cream that early in the day—and Joss was feeling jumpy. Maybe that was due to the coffee, or maybe it was because he hadn't seen his dad yet and wanted to get out of firing range before he did something to upset the man. Either way, he thought it was probably a good idea that he get out the door and get moving.

As he approached the back door, a familiar voice stopped him in his tracks. "Where are you going?"

Henry was standing in the kitchen, hair still damp from a shower, looking bored, but curious. Joss was surprised to see him. Maybe he hadn't slept well in a strange bed. Or maybe he had hoped that no one else would be up, and he could enjoy a moment of quiet before being subjected to his cousin's presence. Joss wondered if Henry had also reflected on the differences in mornings at their houses, and if he was feeling homesick at all because of it. But he wouldn't ask. Mostly because he was feeling homesick enough for Henry's house.

Joss shrugged casually, as if it were the most normal thing in the world. "I'm going to go to Driscoll's ice-cream parlor down the road a bit and get some ice cream."

Henry raised a sharp eyebrow at him then. "For breakfast?"

"Yeah." Joss bit the inside of his cheek. Henry was going to see through his casual trip to the ice-cream parlor for what it really was—reconnaissance for the Slayer Society—and then he was going to get all defensive in the name of Vlad and vampires everywhere. It wasn't a conversation that Joss wanted to have at all. But especially not one he wanted to have on no sleep and hardly any caffeine.

Henry nodded. "I'm in."

"But . . ." But. Joss needed a but. Because Henry couldn't go with him. How was he supposed to investigate a potential crime by vampire with his girl-crazy cousin hanging around? He scrambled for something—anything—to keep Henry from tagging along. "You haven't had breakfast."

Henry slipped his Converse on and tied the laces before meeting Joss's eyes. "Dude, ice cream *is* breakfast."

"How ya figure?" Desperation gave way to panic. He wasn't certain how Henry would react if they got attacked by a vampire. He only knew that it wouldn't be good. For either of them.

"Two words. Bacon. Sundae. Let's go." Henry opened the back door and gestured for Joss to go first. As Joss did, still trying to think of some way to get

Henry to remain behind, Henry lowered his voice so that neither of Joss's parents would hear. "Besides . . . there's no way I'm letting you out of my sight after what you did to my best friend."

An image crept into Joss's mind without his permission. That of blood pouring out onto Joss's palms. Vlad's blood. He blinked it away and met his cousin's gaze with a stern jaw. "What you don't know about that is that I saved him. I saved Vlad's life."

Henry grabbed Joss's shirt collar and yanked him closer. His face was flushing red, and Joss could tell by the way his chest was rising and falling that it was taking every ounce of his cousin's self-control not to strangle him right then and there. Not that Joss blamed him. Not really.

Henry's grip tightened on Joss's shirt until his knuckles turned white. His words were more than a whisper, but just less than a growl. "You *stabbed him* through the heart with a hunk of *wood*."

If it had been anyone besides Henry, Joss would have removed their grip and taught them a good lesson on why they shouldn't invade someone's personal space like that. But this was Henry. They were more like brothers than cousins. And even though it had torn them apart for Henry to learn Joss's darkest secret, he was relieved that Henry had found out. At least that lie wasn't standing between them anymore.

At least, in that sense, anyway, Joss was free. Before he could summon an excuse in his mind, the truth came pouring out of him in whispers, like the rambling of a madman. "I moved it. The stake. I moved it. At the last minute. To the side. So he'd survive. I had to stake him. The Society would have . . . they would have done horrible things if I didn't. But I was willing to make it look like I missed by accident, Henry. Because it's Vlad. He was my friend, too."

Henry winced at the word "friend." His eyes looked furious, but his grip released slightly. And in that moment, Joss saw hope. Hope that maybe someday, somehow, he could make his cousin understand. Maybe they could be friends again. If Henry didn't kill him first, of course.

Henry released him, shoving him back a little with a grunt. "You tried to kill him, Joss. Nothing can change that."

"I *had* to try. It's my *job* to try. It's my *duty* to try." Joss made certain that Henry met his eyes then. He waited for his cousin to look at him, so that Henry could see the absolute sincerity in his gaze. When that moment came, he said, "But I didn't succeed, and I didn't succeed on purpose. He lived, Henry. Vlad lived. Because of me."

The corner of Henry's mouth twitched. It was the only response he gave.

Joss stepped forward, brushing by Henry on his way out the door. Just as he'd stepped outside, Henry stepped out after him. "I'm going with you, Joss. And I'm staying on your every move for the next month, like your new shadow. Because who knows who you might attack if someone's not there to stop you?"

"I'm not going to attack any—" Joss stopped himself before he lied. It was true that he didn't plan on attacking anyone, but what if a vampire attacked him? Then it was all bets off. He didn't want any more lies between his cousin and himself. Shaking his head, he said, "You don't have to follow me. Really."

"Don't have to. But going to. Where's this ice-cream parlor anyway?" Henry stepped outside completely, letting the screen door slap shut behind him.

Joss wasn't exactly sure what to say or what, if anything, he could possibly do to convince Henry that it wasn't the best idea on the planet that he follow Joss around. So rather, he sighed his frustration and shook his head, pointing up the road. "Just up the road a bit."

Henry moved in the direction that Joss had pointed, as if he were leading the way, rather than shadowing Joss's every move. Joss had to jog a little at first in order to catch up with him. When he did, he slowed his pace to match Henry's stride. The two walked in silence for several minutes, until two young boys crossed the road in front of them carrying Nerf guns and sprinting as fast as their small feet would carry them. The sight of it brought a small smile to Joss's face. He dared a glance at Henry, who still wasn't smiling, and bet that Henry might not allow himself even a moment's happiness while he was in the company of Joss McMillan, Vampire Slayer. "That reminds me of the time we snuck up on Greg with Super Soakers."

No response from Henry. Not even a small twitch.

"Do you remember? We filled our squirt guns with cranberry juice and climbed that tree in your backyard. We were going to get him through the open window." Joss chuckled at the memory. "Only it turned out he was supposed to get pictures taken that day and we had no idea."

"My mom was so mad at us." The corner of Henry's mouth lifted in a smirk—one that Joss was enormously relieved to see.

Joss laughed openly, shaking his head. "How were we supposed to know he'd be wearing white?"

"We both got grounded for a week."

"Yeah."

The two cousins exchanged looks then, and Joss wasn't sure what it meant. He only knew that he missed their closeness, their connection. He missed the way that things had been before he'd lost Cecile, before he'd trained to become a Slayer, before he'd staked Vlad. He missed Henry.

Henry blinked, as if bringing himself back to the present. The smile washed from his face, and he turned his attention back to the road. "But that's the past. If I'd known then what you'd turn into later, I—"

"You'd what? There was no stopping this, Henry. I'm a Slayer. It's just a part of me, like having blond hair is a part of you. Like—"

"Like being a vampire is a part of Vlad?" Henry stopped in his tracks then and met Joss's eyes. His words weren't bitter, just matter-of-fact, which in some ways, made them much harder for Joss to hear. "Don't try to make me understand it, Joss. Because I won't ever understand how you think that killing people is like having blond hair. You make choices in life. And you're making the wrong ones."

Joss wanted to blurt out that vampires kill people all the time, much more than Slayers ever do, but instead he fought to keep his mouth shut. An argument at this point in time would get him nowhere. He'd seen the light in Henry's eyes when he spoke of their shared childhood. There was hope there, hope that their friendship could be saved. But he could only save it with patience and time, not with arguments about who had a bigger body count.

Like a beacon, the ice-cream parlor came into view. It was a small building, painted a pale pink color, with crude, childlike drawings of children skipping rope painted on its outer walls. As Joss pushed the door open, a bell jingled, announcing their arrival. No sooner had they approached the young man behind the counter than Henry blurted out, "Superman!"

At first, Joss blinked. Did Henry know this guy or something? Had he seen him out and about in blue tights and red underwear, donning a cape? Or was Henry losing his mind completely?

Henry jabbed a finger at the glass case that covered the enormous cardboard tubs of ice cream. He was pointing at one flavor that looked like the brightest rainbow that Joss had ever seen and grinning at the boy behind the counter. "Superman ice cream. Three scoops. Waffle cone. Make it happen, dude."

A small voice spoke in the back of Joss's mind. *"Not All Superheroes Wear Capes."*

The boy piled three heaping scoops into a waffle cone and handed it to Henry before looking at Joss. He was maybe eighteen, and his eyes looked suspiciously similar to those of the dead owner's. Joss guessed that this was the man's son. He said, "And what can I get you?"

Joss mulled over the ice cream for a bit, trying to think of a casual way to work in questions about the boy's dead father. "Hmmm. It all looks good. Which is your favorite?"

"Moose Tracks. But we're having a sale on Raspberry Bliss."

Joss shrugged and pulled his wallet from his back pocket. "I'll try the raspberry, I guess. Can I ask why it's on sale? It's not, like, bad or anything, is it?"

"Nope. Just doing a little tribute to my dad. It was his favorite flavor." As he spoke, his eyes shimmered. The pain was still fresh, the hurt still new. This was what Henry was missing about Joss's job. Joss was helping people.

As he handed over a ten, Joss frowned. "I'm so sorry. If you don't mind my asking, how did he die?"

"Coyotes, if you can believe it." The boy handed him back his change and sighed, his shoulders slumped in sorrow. He pointed out the window behind him to a spot just across the road. "He was attacked by a small pack of them over there. Just a few yards into the woods. It was strange, too. My dad never went for walks in the woods."

That last sentence sent a curious bolt through Joss. If it was a vampire, it was messy work.

After slipping his change inside, Joss returned his wallet to his pocket, shaking his head the entire time. He might not know what it was like to lose a parent to death, but he could empathize on what it was like to not have your father there for you anymore. And what it was like to lose a close family member. "I'm sorry."

"Me too." The circles under his eyes suggested

that Joss and this boy had more in common that he probably would ever realize. Shutting the cash register drawer, the boy sighed. "Anyway, if you want anything else, just shout. I'll be in the back, doing inventory."

By the time Joss turned his head to look at his cousin, Henry had already devoured half of his ice-cream cone. Joss took two licks of his, just as a measure of politeness, before dropping it in the trash. When Henry cast him a questioning glance, Joss merely shrugged. "Raspberry."

Henry looked at the trash can with an air of disgust. "Gross."

Joss pushed the door open, inciting that jingle once again, and held it for his cousin. Once they were outside, Joss eyed the edge of the tree line, hoping to find something that would definitively tell him whether this was a vampire killing or really just wild animals. He hoped for the latter. "Hey, Henry, I've gotta check out the woods for a second. If you don't mind, I mean."

Henry shoved the last of his ice-cream cone into his mouth. Between chews, he said, "Whatever you say, killer."

The tiny hairs on the back of Joss's neck bristled. But he said nothing in reply.

· 5 ·

A BLAST FROM THE PAST

After waiting for Henry to wipe his face clean with a too-thin napkin and then locate a trash can in which to throw it away, Joss crossed the road and entered the woods, hoping he'd be able to determine where the man who owned the ice-cream parlor, Mr. Driscoll, had died. He was very aware of Henry behind him—his feet tromping over fallen twigs and dead leaves, alerting any vampire within a twenty-mile radius of their presence. Joss understood that Henry hadn't had the benefit of stealth training that the Society had provided him, but he also knew that if a vampire attacked them, he was going to have to save his cousin. After all, Henry was under the mistaken impression that vampires were kind, friendly people who just happened to have fangs and a thirst for blood, but really longed for peace between the species. It likely wouldn't even occur to Henry that vampires were cruel, vicious monsters with an agenda all their own, fighting to drain every human vein they found dry of blood. Henry's brain wasn't wired that way. He'd grown up in a warm, loving household, where people were truly good and life would have a happy ending. Henry grew up not understanding the truth of the world: That it's not always Grandma under the sheet, that the woodsman won't come to save you, and that believing in happy endings will only get you eaten by wolves.

At least, that's how Joss had come to see the world. He knew the truth of things. He understood that sometimes horrible things happen to wonderful families—things that shatter those families into a thousand pieces forever. And that nothing and no one can ever bring those pieces back together ever again. He knew that there really were monsters that lurked in dark places. Monsters with friendly faces. He knew pain, and loss, and absolute fury.

All Henry knew was joy.

Joss hated him for that. And he hated himself for doing so. Just a little bit.

"What are we doing out here?" Henry sighed impatiently behind him.

Joss scanned the area with his keen eyes but saw nothing out of place. It was as if no attack had happened in this location, and he was beginning to wonder if maybe the report of the attack had been a cover-up. "What's the matter, Henry, you don't like hiking?"

Henry stepped up beside him, shrugging. "I'm more of an indoor person most of the time."

Joss glanced at him with a furrowed brow. "What about sports? You and Greg play sports all the time. Aren't those outdoors?"

"Yeah, but we don't run around in the woods for no purpose." Joss was just about to tell Henry that he could see more purpose in hiking through nature than he could in chasing a ball around some field, when Henry asked, "Are you looking for something?"

The woods all around them were quiet and serene. Every once in a while, a critter would dash from one bit of underbrush to the next, but other than that and a few chirpings from the birds in the branches above, the forest was silent. There was no sign of a struggle or footprints or anything that suggested a coyote attack. Joss shrugged. "Kinda. The man who owned the ice-cream shop died out here."

"And you're looking for his body? Gross." Henry's face turned a bit green, but it didn't last.

Joss moved forward and his cousin came with him. As they crested a small hill, Joss said, "No, this guy died a few weeks ago. I'm just curious if it's true what they say about him having been killed by coyotes."

Henry stopped Joss in his tracks with a hand to the chest. "Wait. So you found out that some old dude was ripped to shreds by some coyotes right here and you came out here willingly?"

"Yeah. Basically."

Henry's eyes bugged out of his head. "What if there are still coyotes out here? And what if they're still hungry?"

All Joss could do was shrug. Pretty much because he hadn't really thought that there might still be coyotes out here to deal with. He didn't believe that coyotes had killed the man in the first place. Slayers weren't sent to deal with wild animals. Slayers were sent to eradicate vampires.

"You're either incredibly stupid or incredibly cool." Henry stepped back, shaking his head. The corner of Joss's mouth lifted in a small smile—one that didn't last. Henry put an end to it as quickly as he was able to. "I'm leaning toward option number one."

It bugged Joss that Henry couldn't just enjoy a moment with him, that he had to keep Joss at bay, all because of an incident that had very little to do with him. What had happened between Joss and Vlad was between them. Not Joss's cousin. Not Vlad's drudge. Was it so wrong that he wanted to experience just one moment where they were simply cousins, and not two people on divided sides of an argument? Joss shook his head and went back to surveying the area around them. "Just let me know if you see anything."

"Like blood and guts? Or like vicious wild animals running at me? Because either way, I'm letting you know. Probably with a girlish squeal." Henry looked around at the woods, but Joss didn't see much real worry in his eyes. It was mostly boredom, and irritation at having been dragged into nature unexpectedly.

"I'll have you know that there are some pretty interesting species of insects that feed on corpses."

"You and bugs, man. It's weird." Henry shook his head. Obviously, Joss's love of entomology completely escaped him. Joss would never understand it. Insects made the world go round. They were the planet. They were life. Without them, humans would be nowhere.

Something bold and bright and not at all natural to the forest setting caught Joss's attention. It looked like a bit of cloth or a flag or something. Whatever it was, it was bright yellow and flapping around in the breeze. It looked, from this distance, as if it had caught on some weeds or a branch. Joss moved toward it, happy to have something other than tree trunks and dead leaves to look at. "You see anything out of the ordinary, just let me know."

"So what horrible Slayer task are we here to accomplish, anyway?"

Henry's words stopped Joss dead in his tracks. He turned back to face his cousin. All playfulness was gone from each of their expressions now. Now they were all business. Joss frowned, ready to defend his duty. "I never said we were here on any Slayer business. And if I said that it was?"

Henry set his jaw, the anger and defensiveness already rising up inside of him in an acutely visible way. "I'd kick your—"

"Henry." Joss held up a hand, softening his tone. "I'm just trying to help the kid in that shop by tracking down who or whatever killed his dad. Okay?"

"Yeah, right. I'm not killing anyone. And just so we're clear, when I go back home, I don't plan on speaking to you ever again." Henry walked past him then, even though he hadn't seen the yellow thing, and had no real direction to go in. As he passed Joss, their shoulders hit. He glared at Joss, as if Joss had done it on purpose. In response, Joss simply held up his hands in mock surrender. Henry kept walking.

As Joss approached the bright piece of yellow, he recognized it as a piece of police tape. Crouching, he saw that it hadn't just blown here freely—it was actually tied to a small shrub. The rest of the tape had been ripped away, but Joss was certain that he and his cousin were now standing at the crime scene. Signs of that were all around him. Leaves had been moved away, revealing the forest floor. Small, low hanging branches had been broken free from the surrounding trees. The footsteps of the investigators, and perhaps the victim himself, littered the ground. But the curious thing was that there were no paw prints in the dirt, nothing at all to suggest that a coyote or a group of coyotes had attacked the man at all. If rain had washed away the coyotes' prints, it would have washed away that of the people, too, and it hadn't. So Joss's curiosity level ticked up a notch. Maybe the Society's instincts were right. Maybe a vampire had killed the owner of the ice-cream parlor.

"Why didn't you apologize?" When Joss looked over at his cousin, Henry was standing just a few feet from him, eyes locked on Joss in a way that suggested he wasn't going anywhere until he had the answers he sought. "You could have at least apologized to Vlad after stabbing him with that thing. But he said that even when you came to see him at the hospital, you didn't apologize to him. Why?"

Joss stood his ground, calmly, but firmly. "Because I did nothing wrong."

Disgust visibly washed over Henry. "You put a stake through his internal organs, Joss. You nearly killed him. That, at least, deserves an apology."

"Do soldiers apologize when they take down a terrorist? No. Because they did nothing wrong. They're just following orders by taking out a threat to innocent people. Which is what I was doing." Joss was trying everything that he could to keep his voice calm and even, but it was a challenge. Henry was acting like he was some terrible villain, like he was the Joker, when clearly, he was Batman.

Henry stepped closer and dropped his voice to a near-whisper, holding Joss's gaze as he spoke. "Have you ever stopped to think about who's giving you those orders? What if you're mindlessly obeying the instructions of the bad guys?"

Joss shook his head, clenching his jaw. "The Slayer Society is noble and right and good, Henry. You have no idea what you're talking about. They're good people."

"Vlad's a good person." Henry tilted his head. He'd never listen to Joss. He'd never listen to reason. And it was seriously ticking Joss off.

Without thinking, Joss gave Henry a light shove and then pointed a finger at him angrily. "You only think that because he's got you under his spell. Your mind is lost in a vampire-induced haze. You're his human slave, Henry!"

At that, Henry balled his fist and as he brought it up, Joss dodged out of the way. But it wouldn't have mattered if Joss had stayed right where he was, because something moved out of the surrounding forest and whipped past Joss's face, carrying Henry with it. In a blink, Joss saw his cousin slam against the trunk of a white birch tree. His eyes rolled over white, and Henry slid down the trunk of the tree in an unconscious heap.

Joss immediately reached for the leather holster that was hidden on his hip, beneath his shirt. But before he could grip his stake, the creature rushed by again, knocking the wooden weapon away before he could grab it. Joss scrambled, spinning around, trying to locate his missing stake and get a look at whatever it was that had attacked his cousin and then disarmed him. But he couldn't see the creature anywhere.

Which told him that this wasn't just some lightning-quick animal. This was a vampire.

Joss braced himself for anything and reached up, snapping loose a section of low-hanging branch. The wood was dead, but solid enough to work. He listened to the sounds of the forest for anything that stood out as unusual. Breathing, footsteps, anything. But there was nothing.

From nowhere, Joss was slammed against the tree, his head bouncing off of its trunk. The sharp section of branch was ripped from his hand. And when he looked at what it was that had pinned him, his heart sank. His throat closed with heartbreak and sorrow. His entire being filled with confusion. The fight had left him—something that filled him with shame as well. Because a Slayer should fight. A Slayer would fight. Especially in this situation.

The eyes were just as kind, just as sympathetic as Joss could remember. The mouth—Joss couldn't look at it for long, due to the horrible fangs inside—was the same. Everything about him was the same as the last time that they had spoken. The lines in the face no worse, as the man was now frozen in time. A vampire. Forever. And there was nothing that Joss could do to reverse his condition. When Joss spoke at last, his voice came out shaking from utter shock. "Sirus?"

Sirus nodded slowly. He looked to be sizing up how much danger he was in. Joss shook his head, not knowing if what he was seeing was real, or some twisted image his sleep-starved brain had conjured. "Sirus? I thought you died. That explosion. I thought I—"

"You didn't kill me, Joss, but you did do a lot of damage." Sirus relaxed his grip on Joss, and gave a small, grateful smile. Joss could only assume that Sirus was grateful that Joss had engaged him with words rather than combat. When Sirus smiled, it broke Joss's heart a little bit more. Sirus said, "It's good to see you, too."

Joss had so many questions, he didn't know where to begin. Sirus had survived the explosion in the cabin? How? And what was he doing here now? Where was Kat? Did she know her father was still alive? What was he here to do exactly? The questions jumbled around in his mind, until they were all just a big blur. He stammered. "H-h-h-how?"

"Joss, I'm sorry about your cousin, and about your head, but I don't have much time and I had to get him out of the way and you unarmed. I'm here to warn you. There's . . . something in the woods. It's coming for you. And it's far worse than Em." Sirus looked sharply to his left then, deeper into the woods. The look in his eyes was one of sheer panic.

Joss glanced around, but saw nothing. "How do you know that? And how do you know that Em's after me?"

Henry moaned softly from where he lay at the base of the tree. Slowly, he was stirring into wakefulness, but he wasn't quite there yet.

"Listen to me." Sirus pressed him against the tree again, with more force than Joss wagered he'd intended. It was his vampire strength—probably difficult to control. Sirus moved so close that Joss had a brief worry that he might bite. Instead, Sirus gripped Joss's collar with one hand and pressed his stake into his palm with the other. His words were those of absolute sincerity. "Trust your dreams. They're more real than you realize."

"How did you know where to find me?" Silently, Joss swore not to report this part to the Society. Not yet. He needed some time to wrap his head around the strangeness of it all, and to make certain that he hadn't lost his mind entirely.

Sirus smiled again, and oh, how Joss hated that his heart lit up to see it. Sirus. Still alive. It was a miracle. "We share a friend who told me where to find you. By the way, Dorian sends his greetings. He says he looks forward to seeing you again."

Then, in a light breeze, Sirus was gone. The stake felt heavy in Joss's hand. He spun around, searching the trees for any sign of his long-lost friend. "When will I see you again? I have things to ask you! Sirus? Sirus? Sirus!"

But Sirus was gone.

▸·6·◂

THE FRAGILE LIAR

J oss brought the ax down hard, splitting another log, this time with ease. As he did so, he was reminded of his initial Slayer training, and how horrible that summer in the Catskills had been for him. It was for the good of the cause, he supposed, but it was difficult to see while he was in the moment, and if he was honest, even more difficult to see as time passed by. But he wasn't really thinking about the Slayer Society at all as he chopped firewood for his dad, who thought that they should probably get things ready for the coming fall and winter, even though summer had only just barely started. Instead, he was thinking about Sirus, and about what he probably should have done when he saw Sirus, but didn't. And why he didn't.

He should have killed Sirus. He knew that. But he hadn't acted on it.

The truth was, when he saw Sirus's face and had realized that his mentor, his friend, his father figure was still alive, he was relieved. More relieved, maybe, than when he'd seen Vlad, lying in the hospital, and had learned that he'd survived as well. Because Vlad had been his friend, but Sirus had been his . . . well . . . like a dad to him. Guiltily, he glanced at the house in the growing darkness. He probably shouldn't think that way, or feel that way, or be that way, but there it was. Sirus had been a kinder, more attentive father than his own dad had been capable of in recent years. And despite those damned fangs in his mouth, Joss had been utterly overjoyed at seeing him once again.

Joss stuck the blade into a nearby log and stood back, wiping his neck with a handkerchief and feeling like the worst son in existence. He hated that he liked Sirus better than his own dad. But how do you change the way that you feel? Isn't something like that ingrained on your heart, if not your DNA? After shoving the handkerchief half into his back jeans pocket once again, Joss retrieved the ax and set up another log. As he lifted the tool, his thoughts drifted to Henry.

Once Sirus had disappeared into the woods, Joss shook Henry into consciousness and helped him to stand. The entire walk home, Henry was in a daze and holding his head. Joss wasn't sure what to say to his cousin about what exactly had slammed him against that tree, so he said nothing about it at all. Once they returned home, Henry went in the guest room and Joss was given chores all day. They hadn't spoken since. Joss was kind of relieved about that.

After all, how do you explain to your vampire-adoring cousin that a vampire just knocked the snot out of him without provocation? You don't. You just chop some wood and hope the whole thing blows over in time for dinner.

As if on cue, the side door opened and Henry stepped outside. Joss brought the ax down again before tossing the split log neatly into the pile to his left. He was hoping, praying, counting on Henry not approaching him, not saying a word, and if he had to speak, to not ask about what had knocked him out in the woods. Mostly because he already knew where that conversation would lead, and he absolutely didn't want to go there with his cousin again. Why couldn't they stick to simple discussion topics, like the weather or which hot celebrity Henry unrealistically thought he had a chance at? Why did it always have to be about vampires?

A small voice spoke up from the back of Joss's mind. One he wished that he couldn't hear. It said that Joss had it wrong. His way of thinking was askew. It wasn't about vampires at all—not for Henry. For Henry, it was about his best friend, plain and simple. Vampire or human—it didn't matter to Henry. Vlad was his friend. And Joss had almost killed him.

Joss reminded the voice that he was a Slayer, and that it was his job to kill vampires.

Inside his imagination, the voice just gave him a knowing look. One that caused Joss to sigh deeply as he reached for the next log.

Henry's shoulders were slightly slumped as he approached. "I'm supposed to help you with the wood." Clearly, the last thing that he wanted to be doing was hanging out in the growing darkness with his cousin, chopping wood. Come to think of it, that was the last thing that Joss wanted, too. "Your dad said he wants it done by dinner."

Dinner. The world rolled around uncomfortably inside Joss's mind, like a loose marble. He was so used to grabbing a sandwich by himself or popping a frozen meal into the microwave that he was pretty uncertain what Henry had meant by his dad mentioning the *D* word. Dinner was something that their family had had before they lost Cecile. Now they simply foraged in the kitchen for food while avoiding eye contact. "What's for dinner?"

"Pizza." He and Henry locked eyes then. Joss hated what he saw on Henry's face, but it was undeniable. Pity. Henry couldn't deny what was lying all around him in shambles. Joss's family was falling apart, and now he knew that for sure.

Joss stood there, the ax dangling in his right hand, shifting his feet uncomfortably in embarrassment. He could feel tears beginning to well in his eyes but fought to keep them contained. "Remember how much my mom loved to cook? Before?"

He hadn't been able to say "Before Cecile died," but he knew Henry would understand what he'd meant. It was too difficult to talk about his sister. Especially when discussing the chaos and destruction that had been left in the wake of her demise.

Henry forced a smile, his eyes shimmering. "Yeah. She and my mom could cook circles around each other. But . . . things change, I guess."

"I hope they don't." Henry tilted his head curiously at Joss's words, so Joss clarified. "I mean, I hope that my mom's love of cooking is still in there somewhere. I keep on hoping that I'll wake up to the smells of breakfast and happiness, y'know?"

Memories of his mom's creativity in the kitchen

came flooding through Joss's mind. The table had always been perfectly set. The food was in abundance, and the recipes wonderfully complex. His mom had had a passion for cooking then. And now she didn't have a passion for anything. She took her medication and sat quietly most of the time, the color drained from her days. Joss worried about her. He worried a lot, and with good reason.

"Losing Cecile really changed things, didn't it? The extended family talks, of course, and I see it when you guys visit, but I really had no idea how bad it had gotten for your family, Joss. You all just seem so . . ." Henry swallowed hard, wiping his eyes with the back of his hand. His words were softly spoken and carefully chosen. ". . . fragile."

Fragile. Meaning they could be broken. Joss refused to believe that, refused to believe that his family could crumble and blow away with the wind. He tightened his grip on the ax and readied another log, his jaw tight, his shoulders newly tense. He never should have talked to Henry about this, never should have opened himself up in this way. What good could possibly come of it? Nothing. "We're fine."

"You don't have to—"

"I said we're fine." Joss brought the ax down hard, cutting both the wood and Henry's words. Clearly, Henry had hit a nerve.

Henry watched him quietly for several minutes as Joss moved through several logs. Just as the sun had finally dipped behind the trees, casting a nighttime feel, Henry spoke. His tone was even, as if he were worried that any misspeak might damage the already frazzled Joss. Joss would never admit it if asked, but he was right. "What can I do to help?"

Joss lowered the ax momentarily and looked around before pointing to the house. "Carry the wood I've already cut over to the rack by the garage and stack it."

Without complaint, Henry moved from the cut pile to the stack by the garage and back again. Joss continued to cut wood, all the while amazed at how cooperative his normally hotheaded cousin was being.

"My head's still killing me." Henry rubbed his temples as he approached the last few logs in the cut pile. Then, as if remembering something, he paused and looked at Joss. "Hey, what happened out there today? Was it a coyote or something? What hit me?"

Joss furrowed his brow in contemplation. On one hand, it was actually kinda nice to have someone to talk to about the existence of vampires. On the other, he knew that admitting anything regarding a vampire attack would put Henry immediately on the defensive. Joss made an executive decision and looked at his cousin. "It was a coyote. Big one, too. After it hit you, it ran off deeper into the woods. Apparently it thought you were alone. When it saw there were two of us, it must have gotten spooked. We were lucky. Looks like that guy died by a coyote attack after all."

Instantly, Joss could tell that Henry didn't believe a word that he was saying. And who could blame him? Joss's tone was so full of it, he might as well have had a sign on his forehead flashing "I AM SUCH A LIAR" in bright neon red. But it wasn't Joss's fault. He was having a difficult time focusing on being smooth and believable on the heels of the discussion about his "fragile" family. In short, he wasn't trying hard enough. And they both knew it.

Henry raised an eyebrow. "Are you lying to me?"

"No." Joss's heart beat hard inside his chest, as if tapping him in quiet disagreement.

"You're lying to me." It wasn't a question anymore. Not that it had been much of one in the first place, but Henry had been giving him a chance then. Now there was no turning back.

"No, I'm not." Joss set his jaw stubbornly.

"Joss."

"What?"

Henry groaned, running a haphazard hand through his hair. Astoundingly, his hair looked even better after. He met Joss's eyes and visibly fought to keep his tone calm. "Was it a vampire?"

He wanted to shout that yes, yes, it was a vampire, and that vampire was someone near and dear to him, and he was so confused at this point about how exactly he was supposed to feel about it that he felt like imploding . . . but he couldn't. Because that would mean that the Society might be wrong about vampires. And that Henry might be right about Vlad.

Joss stuck the ax into an oversized log then and shook his head. "I don't know what you're talking about."

Henry looked more irritated than Joss had ever seen him. He was holding it together surprisingly well. Joss wondered how long his calm demeanor could possibly last. Henry's eyes widened as Joss stepped past him toward the house. He placed a hand on Joss's shoulder, stopping him. "Dude, if a vampire attacked me, I have a right to know."

Joss shook him off, more roughly than he needed to. "And if I said it was a vampire, what then? Would you defend them then?"

"Of course not. They're not all good. No group of any kind of person is all good." Henry stood there, demanding Joss's attention, his eyes full of a fire that threatened to spread wildly. But he looked like he was desperately trying to prevent it from doing so. Only Joss couldn't understand why. "So?"

Joss threw his arms up. He was raising his voice to

a near shout, but couldn't stop himself. So much anger and guilt and remorse and embarrassment was filling him that Joss thought that he might just explode into a cloud of ash. "Yes. Yes, okay? A vampire knocked you unconscious!"

He shoved Henry back with both palms, hard. Henry stumbled, but righted himself immediately. "Why are you getting so ticked off?"

Because Henry was here, asking him questions about things he didn't want to talk about. Because Sirus was alive and a vampire and not his real dad. Because his family was in shambles, and no amount of pretending could hide that fact from the world. Because his sister was dead, and it was his job to avenge her. Joss was mad for all of these reasons and more. But worse than any of that, he was losing it completely. He had to get away from Henry and regain his composure before he did or said something really stupid.

As if a light had gone on over Henry's head, he said, "Did you kill him?"

In Joss's mind, he saw the cabin from two summers ago exploding, the flames and debris flying outward. Then he saw Sirus's face as it had been just a few hours ago in the woods. His smile, still so kind, still so warm. His heart regretted feeling the elation that it had at the sight of him, but it was undeniable that he had felt it. Stunned at his own confusion, Joss slowly shook his head. "No. No, I didn't kill it."

"So he got away. No wonder you're mad."

"I'm not mad and . . ." He shook his head. He was so tired of lying, but it felt like the only way out. "Yeah, basically, it got away."

Henry folded his arms across his chest. "Basically. Hmm."

"Let's just get inside and eat some pizza, okay? I really don't feel like talking to you about vampires anymore." Joss started back toward the house, his thoughts racing. Why was his cousin doing this? This was all Henry's fault. If Henry hadn't been asking so many stupid questions, Joss wouldn't have to think about Sirus or his family or anything unpleasant that was going on. He would still be lost in the mundane task of chopping wood. Overwhelmed, he spun around and shoved Henry again. "Why can't you just admit how dangerous they are?"

Henry shoved him back, his words right on the heels of his action. "I thought you didn't want to talk about them anymore!"

"Well, now I do! Why, Henry?"

"Nope. Sorry. We're done." Henry brushed past him. "You don't want to talk anymore? That's fine. Or maybe you could kiss my—"

Joss grabbed his cousin by the shirt. It was only after he'd balled up his fist that he realized that he meant to hurt Henry. Slowly, he lowered his hand and released his cousin, who looked as if his temper had been pushed to the absolute brink. But, try as Joss might to change it, his tone was still full of venom. "Why?"

Henry shook his head, like Joss were a sad, pathetic person who was blind to the ways of the world. Joss instantly despised him for it and immediately regretted that emotion. "Because they're not all dangerous. They're not all good or all bad. You seem to think that the word *vampire* is the same as the word *evil*, and that's not true."

Joss shook his head. He wasn't the blind one here. "And you seem to think that the word *Slayer* and the word *murderer* are one in the same, and that's not true. I'm defending mankind with my actions. Things aren't always what they seem, Henry."

There was a moment when neither spoke. But it wouldn't last. It couldn't last.

Henry made his way to the side door, and as he opened it he turned back to face his cousin. "That's exactly the point I've been trying to make about Vlad. Things aren't what they seem. When are you gonna realize that?"

As the screen door slapped closed behind Henry, Joss shouted, "When are *you*?"

As he stood there in the growing darkness, Joss realized two things. One, he was growing ever certain that he and his cousin would never again be as close as they once were. And two, if Henry was going to survive the next month in a town where vampires were roaming free, Joss was going to have to keep him close.

Oh yes, he thought as he moved toward his house and the smell of pepperoni pizza within. The Slayer Society was going to love this plan.

· 7 ·

CECILE'S EYES

It was a noise that woke him that night, though in his half-conscious state, it was difficult for Joss to remember exactly what that noise had been. Curiosity, more than alarm, kept him wondering, kept him guessing, and finally, Joss opened his eyes. His bedroom was empty, as far as he could see in the darkness. No stray animals, no unexpected guests. Just him, his stuff, and the cool breeze blowing his curtains farther into the room.

He relaxed back into his mattress and had just sighed a sleepy, relieved sigh when he heard the noise again. It sounded like the creaking of floorboards. Joss tried to ignore it. Maybe it was just the house settling.

Then he heard it again. *Creeeeak . . .*

Wide awake at the sound, Joss listened to his heart hammer in his ears. He was ashamed of himself instantly. What kind of Slayer hides under his covers at the first discovery of some unexplainable noise? It was ridiculous. Slowly, he pushed the sheet back from his legs and sat up on the edge of his bed, looking around.

Nothing. Just his room. Just his stuff. Just the breeze.

Feeling more than a little stupid, Joss cursed himself for being so needlessly on edge. He was just about to slip back under his covers when he heard it again. *Creeeeak . . .*

Joss's heart immediately picked up its pace. It was coming from down the hall. More specifically than that, it sounded like it was coming from Henry's room.

With his stake gripped firmly in his hand, Joss opened his bedroom door and crept down the hall. As he pushed Henry's partially open door open even more, he thought about the night that he had lost Cecile. He remembered it like it was yesterday. He'd been awoken by a sound in the middle of the night. He'd crept down the hall to his baby sister's room, and when he peered inside her open door, he saw a vampire looming over her sleeping form.

Only she wasn't sleeping. Cecile was dead.

He pushed the door open and what he saw sent his heart into his throat. Someone was standing beside Henry's bed, looking down on him. At first, Joss couldn't focus on who or what it was that was standing there. He could only stare at his cousin and wait for any sign that Henry was still alive.

When Henry's chest rose in a deep breath, Joss sighed in relief. But there was still the other matter. An invader was standing in his home, just inches from his unguarded cousin. Joss readied his weapon and stepped into the room, closing the door behind him.

Only then did he recognize who was standing in the dark of Henry's room. Her blond, curly hair was unmistakable, and Joss knew that if she looked at him, it would be with black, tunnel eyes. He was dreaming. He had to be dreaming. It was Cecile. And he only ever saw Cecile in his dreams.

Recalling his former nightmares, Joss was hesitant to ask her what she was doing here. He didn't want an answer, didn't want to know. Because sooner or later, this dream Cecile would try to kill him, and Joss just couldn't bear it anymore. So instead he stood there in the darkness, watching the way the breeze brushed her hair back from her face. He wished that she'd look at him then, and when she did that he'd see her pretty blue eyes. But those were gone. Only filthy, black tunnels remained in their stead—he knew that much.

Only this nightmarish version of Cecile remained, because his Cecile, his cherub of a sister, was gone. Forever gone. And it was all Joss's fault.

Refusing to speak, to engage her in any way, Joss just stood there silently and looked at her, waiting for something horrible to happen. But when she turned her head toward him, something was very different from his other nightmares about Cecile. Her fingers weren't filthy claws. Her hair wasn't half covering her face. And her eyes . . .

Even in the dark of night, he could see that they were blue.

She looked sad as she watched him, and Joss couldn't resist taking a step toward her. This nightmare was unlike any that had come before it. They had all felt incredibly real, but in this one, Cecile seemed different somehow. More present. Joss debated speaking to her, but what would he say?

Just as he'd decided to ask her what she was doing here, what she wanted from him, and if she could ever find it in her restless heart to forgive him for having failed to save her life, Cecile stepped closer to Henry's bed. Joss hesitated, fearful of what might happen. When nothing did, he parted his lips to speak. But it was Cecile who spoke, instead. In a hushed, child's whisper, she said, "This was my bed."

Joss looked at the guest room bed. She was right. It

was the same frame that she used to sleep on. It was, technically, Cecile's old bed. His parents had kept the frame, painted it, and created a guest room that almost never had guests.

Joss glanced at his sleeping cousin. A line of drool ran from Henry's mouth to the sheets. It reminded Joss of the line of blood that had run from Cecile's mouth to her sheets. The scenes were strangely similar.

"Go back to sleep, Jossie."

Sleep? What on earth could she mean by that? Did she want him to sleep? Was that even possible to do within a dream? Or was she telling him to sleep more, to face her nightmarish images, to stop running from his rest so that he might escape her? He was about to ask what she meant, but the words were stolen from his throat when Cecile opened her mouth. Inside were two perfect, white fangs. Once again, his sister was a monster. Once again, she was a reminder of his absolute failure. She shouted, "Sleep! Now!"

Darkness overtook him, swirling in around him like liquid. He bolted up in bed, and as he brought his hand from underneath his pillow, he realized that he was gripping his stake so tightly that his hand ached. In his half-asleep state, he jumped from his bed, searching his room for any sign of the nightmare that was his younger sister. Of course there was nothing. Of course. Because it had all just been another bad dream. They would never stop. He would never be free of this guilt.

Joss turned to climb back into bed, back under the comfort of his covers, but stopped, frozen in place. His bedroom window, which he was certain had been open when he went to bed the first time, was now closed.

As Joss stood there, his fingers trembling, his heartbeat racing in fear and wonder, Sirus's words echoed through his memory. *"Trust your dreams."*

▸ 8 ◂

AT LONG LAST

After tossing and turning for much of the night—and trying to recall whether his window had actually been open when he went to bed or if he was simply misremembering—Joss finally crawled out of bed with the reluctance of someone who could have used another six or seven hours of sleep. He stretched his arms overhead, reveling in how great it made the muscles in his back feel, then scratched his head and yawned. There was no denying it. It was morning. Might as well face the inevitable.

He was incredibly surprised, given the time, that his dad hadn't yet screamed him out of bed, but at the same time, Joss was relieved. For once, he'd been allowed to sleep in. If only he'd actually been able to, y'know, sleep.

He grabbed some clean clothes and hurried through a shower. Today he was planning to visit the family home of the second person on his list. It was so strange to work on a case for the Slayer Society without the help of his fellow Slayers. And stranger still to be working on a case here at home. It almost felt like he wasn't acting as a Slayer at all. It felt as if the presence of Sirus had been no more real than the dream he'd had about Cecile. It felt as if his past, his memories were chasing him like shadows. Not at all like he was actively investigating the mysterious deaths of four people. Joss looked at his reflection and frowned. He needed to take his job more seriously. He needed to hunt down the killer or killers of these people and determine whether or not they're vampires. And he needed to do it before another name was added to the list.

As he brushed his teeth, he tilted his head at his reflection in contemplation. Sirus was a vampire. What if these murders were all Sirus's handiwork? It was possible, he thought as he spat in the sink and rinsed his toothbrush in the running water. Anything was possible.

So maybe Sirus was the killer. And maybe still,

Joss would have to take his life at some point. Even though he desperately didn't want to—something he could never, ever admit to anyone.

According to the Slayer Society, it was his duty as a Slayer to kill all vampires—first and foremost those that have proven to be an immediate threat to humans. The simple truth was that Sirus was a vampire. Sirus was a threat to humans. No matter how else that Joss might feel about him. Therefore, it was Joss's job to kill Sirus. His duty. His mission in life. To not kill Sirus would be a huge insult to the Society and all that it stood for. The same way that it had been an insult to the Society for Vlad to be allowed to live. The fact that Vlad still lived troubled Joss.

So why was Joss even considering letting Sirus live?

He placed his palms on either side of the sink and let his head drop with a heavy sigh. He didn't know. He didn't know why he couldn't just do his job and move on to the next one. He didn't know why it meant so much to him to see Sirus's smile, or to know that he'd survived that explosion. He just knew that those things had mattered to him, and that the Society would frown on that.

As he raised his head, he didn't meet his reflection's eyes. He couldn't.

He tidied up the mess he'd made in the bathroom before heading downstairs to the kitchen, where his mother was sitting quietly. On the table in front of her were three bottles of medication. Beside that was her half-empty mug of black coffee. She was still wearing her robe, her hair—curly like Cecile's—still looking wild, as if she'd only gotten out of bed a few minutes before. Joss wondered if she was sleeping well at night, or if she was having nightmares, too. He wondered a lot of things about his mother, but was afraid to ask.

After heating up a Pop-Tart, and eating half of it, he took a seat across from her at the table. "Morning, Mom."

She blinked before smiling at him, as if she had only just now become aware that her son had entered the room. "Oh, Joss. Good morning. Did you have breakfast yet?"

He glanced at his plate. "Yeah."

It wasn't her fault that she was lost in her own world half the time. It was her depression. It was her medication. It was her sorrow. Joss didn't blame her for any of it.

Eyeing the prescription bottles, Joss took another bite of his Pop-Tart and said, "Do those things really make you feel better?"

At first, she didn't answer. Then, as if realizing

▾ 93 ▾

that her son had been speaking to her and not his breakfast, she said, "Hmm? Oh, the pills? Sometimes, I think. Sometimes I wonder."

Sometimes Joss wondered, too. He believed in the importance of medication and the treatment of depression, but it was difficult to see if all of these pills were good for his mom. "Hey, Mom. I know this sounds stupid. But I have to say it. Because I don't know if any of those doctors have told you or not." He furrowed his brow, uncertain whether or not he was doing the right thing. Then he placed a hand on hers and squeezed. When she met his eyes, he said, "It's okay to feel sad. Sometimes I feel sad, too. Sometimes I feel so sad about . . . about what happened to Cecile . . . that I don't know if I can bear another day going by without her. But then I remember that the sadness can't last forever, and I can face another day. Maybe we have to experience sadness to truly appreciate the good stuff, y'know?"

He didn't want to see it, but halfway through his statement, his mom's eyes fogged over. He'd lost her again. To the pills. To the pain. To something that he couldn't even hope to control. He'd lost his mom, and it was almost worse than losing Cecile.

She blinked at him once again. "Do you want some breakfast?"

His heart felt heavy. As he stood to rinse his plate off in the sink, he said, "No, thanks."

His mom went back to sipping her coffee. He wondered what it must be like inside the protective world that she'd built all around herself on the day that Cecile had died. He hoped it was a pleasant place, and that she could find some semblance of happiness and peace there. In the way that she couldn't out here in the real world.

Joss glanced longingly at the coffeemaker before speaking again. "Is Henry up yet?"

In that distracted, overly medicated way that she had of speaking, she said, "There was a notice on the door. It said there was a package at the post office. Before he left for work, your father asked Henry to pick it up."

Joss nodded. He really wanted to start investigating the details of the next victim's death, but couldn't really do so without worrying that Henry was finding trouble somewhere. Largely, trouble with fangs. "Do you know when he'll be back?"

"Not for a while, I imagine." She blinked, remembering. The fog lifted briefly from her eyes. "He called, just a minute ago. He met a girl, so they're grabbing breakfast together at that little café on the boardwalk."

Joss shook his head. Henry had been in town for

just a few days and he was already hooking up with some girl. Some things never changed. "What café?"

"Next to the comic book shop. You know the one. That nice man, Edgar Frog, owns it."

Joss immediately rolled his eyes. Edgar Frog was a nut job who'd inherited the comic book shop from his parents. He claimed quite publicly that his brother had been taken by vampires and that he, in fact, was a vampire killer for hire. The guy was nuts and wouldn't know a real Slayer if one staked him through the chest.

After placing his plate in the sink, Joss refilled his mom's coffee mug and headed back upstairs. He had to trust that his cousin was remotely safe on the board-walk, far away from the woods. And his dad was off at work, giving Joss a few hours of peace and quiet. So it was time to do a little research on the woman who'd died in a rather unusual manner. He headed upstairs to his bedroom, hit the power button on his laptop, and got to work.

After an hour of research, Joss had focused in on two important facts. One, the woman died at her house, which was located close to the very boardwalk that his cousin was currently hanging out at. And two, the woman had apparently died in a freak acci-dent involving her falling on her gardening shears and almost beheading herself. Joss sat back after he'd read that last little tidbit over and over again. What person was stupid enough to believe that that woman's death could be anything other than the result of a vampire encounter? It seemed so obvious to Joss. But then, maybe that was just how Joss's brain was wired.

Of course, her husband may have killed her. Crazy people did crazy things. With gardening shears, apparently.

He powered down his laptop and closed it, debating whether he should investigate the crime scene first or check on Henry. With any luck, Henry was in good hands—cute, manicured hands—so he made a decision and grabbed his backpack, feeling better already at the heft of it on his shoulder. Inside was his Slayer kit, and everything that he needed to take down a vampire, in case he ran into one. All but his stake, which he wore in the leather holster on his hip, tucked secretly beneath the fabric of his shirt. He headed downstairs and outside, ready to check out the woman's house. Or more specifically, her garden, where she'd died.

It didn't take him long to reach the dead woman's house, and when he got there, it seemed to be the opposite of gloom, the antithesis of what someone might think of when they thought about a murder scene. The house itself was painted a pretty shade of yellow, with bright white trim. Lush gardens surrounded it, encased by a white picket fence. A quaint cobblestone walkway led from the gate at the sidewalk up to the front door, where large hanging ferns lined the large porch. The home was a place of happiness—that much was obvious. So he wondered if new owners had taken over, or if the woman's husband, who'd been mentioned in the articles that Joss had read, was still living here.

He thought it might be better if her husband had no idea why Joss was there. Pushing the gate open, Joss crept through and moved to the window closest to the walkway. He thought if he could get a peek at whether or not anyone was home, it might be easier to really search the garden, to determine if there were any other remaining details that would solidify his vampire theory. To his relief, when he looked through the window, he saw no one. Then Joss turned around to find a very large, very angry-looking man wearing bib overalls and staring at him as if he were a criminal. In a way, Joss supposed, he was. He was technically trespassing, after all.

The man grunted. "Who are you? What do you want? What are you doing out here?"

Joss immediately plastered a pleasant, apologetic smile on his face. "I'm so sorry. My name's Harry. Harry Bossmire. I'm in the horticulture club at my school, and as I was walking by, I noticed your lovely garden. I rang the bell, but I guess you didn't hear it. I was hoping to talk to whoever planted all of this."

Joss was surprised by how easily the lie had formed in his mind and exited his mouth. Now his only hope was that the man had bought it. That would be the true test.

By the look on the man's face, Joss was willing to bet that he didn't believe a word of what Joss was saying. There was no telling how this conversation would go, but at the moment, Joss was just hoping to leave with his head still attached.

After a long silence, during which the man eyed Joss suspiciously, he grunted again. "That would be my wife. She passed on about a week ago, though. Sorry I can't help you."

Joss shook his head, frowning. On one hand, he was relieved the guy had bought his story. On the other, he felt bad for him. He hated to lie, but his sympathy, at least, was real. "Oh, I'm so sorry. If I had had any idea, I wouldn't have brought it up."

"That's okay, boy. How were you to know?" He shrugged, and when he did, his eyes glistened. This man wasn't a psycho. This man was in mourning. "Tilly loved her flowers. She spent hours out here every day, pruning, watering, making everything just so."

It was clear by the look in his eye that he'd loved that aspect of his wife's personality. She sounded like she was nurturing and caring. And he looked like he missed her more than anybody could ever possibly understand.

"It was an accident, what happened to Tilly. I found her over there by the side of the house, lying sprawled out by the creeping ivy. I wanted to bury her by the violets near the back door, but there are laws, y'know." He nodded to himself, his face drawn and sad. Joss was certain that he'd never seen anyone look so alone before. "Anyway, I just water 'em now. Don't know really much about gardening. Sorry I can't help you."

Before Joss could say anything more, the man moved up the steps to the porch and opened his door, ready to disappear into his house. He probably wasn't used to sharing his grief with the world, and Joss had forced his way in and made him do it. Joss felt terrible. He called after the man, "That's okay. I'm sorry about your wife."

"Feel free to pick some flowers for your club. Tilly would have liked that." The man waved and went inside. As Joss made his way back out the gate, he felt like a real tool. There had to have been a better, gentler way of handling that kind of situation. He just wasn't certain what that was.

He turned his head back to the house and glimpsed the ivy, where Tilly's husband had found her body. Briefly, he wondered whether or not her body had been drained of blood, and if such a thing might be noted under her cause of death by the coroner. Again, that word—messy—filled his head. If a vampire had killed Tilly, it wasn't an experienced one. It was one acting out of desperation, out of intense hunger.

He thought about Tilly, and about her husband, all the way to the café.

As he passed by Frog Brothers Comic Book Shop, Joss glanced inside. He could see Edgar in there, touting some dramatic tale of creatures with fangs to several tourists. Joss just rolled his eyes and kept walking. Amateurs.

The small café next door seemed to be bustling with activity, and Joss wondered if Henry would even still be inside or if he'd taken too long talking to Tilly's husband. But as he stepped inside, he immediately spied Henry sitting in a booth at the far end of the café. Sitting across from him was a very pretty girl, her hair dyed in a rainbow of bright, unnatural colors. She was dressed in combat boots, fishnet tights, black shorts, and a T-shirt. And as Joss approached, he felt every single one of the alarm bells in his brain go off simultaneously.

She glanced over at him when he reached the booth and smiled. All he could do was stare.

Henry looked at Joss and gestured to his new friend. "Oh, hey, Joss. This is Kat."

As he locked eyes with Kat, with Sirus's daughter,

with his sworn enemy, Joss's heart seized inside his chest. The only words he could think to speak were "I know."

Kat smiled at him. Whether it was because she was happy to see him after so long, or because she was poised to kill him momentarily, he had no idea. He just knew that she was here. After years of threatening his life, and of seeking vengeance for her father's untimely demise at Joss's hand . . . Kat was in Santa Carla. Sharing an oversized breakfast burrito with Henry McMillan.

· 9 ·

THERE ARE WORSE THINGS

"**W**hat do you mean you know? You two know each other?" Henry looked more than a little irritated, like Joss was trying to hedge in on his territory with the cute girl he'd just met. His concerns couldn't be further from the truth, of course—Joss was more worried about Kat killing him than kissing him—but Henry had no way of knowing that.

"Oh, Joss and I go way back. I've actually been counting the days till I saw him again. Bet he's been *dying* to run into me." The edges of her smile curled a bit, and Joss's head ached from the amount of tension in his spine. He knew what she was doing. She was trying to intimidate him. But it wasn't going to work. Because he wasn't going to let it work. People can only really bother you if you let them.

"What have you been up to Kat?" He left off the part where he asked if she'd been stalking him in any other way but by text message. Briefly, he wondered if she had texted him since his dad had confiscated his cell phone. But he didn't ask. He wasn't that curious about anything that Kat did or didn't do.

She raised a perfectly manicured eyebrow at him, and Joss couldn't help but notice how incredibly hot Kat had become since he'd last seen her. Ironically, her T-shirt read COOL CHICK on the front. She leaned forward, holding his gaze. Against his will, he wondered if she thought he'd gotten better looking, too. "I could ask the same of you, Joss. The only difference is that I know what *you've* been up to. The question is . . . does Henry?"

It was a threat, plain and simple. It didn't make any difference at all that the threat was coming out of pretty, glossed, perfectly kissable Cupid's bow lips. Joss glared at her. "Henry knows as much as he needs to know about my comings and goings."

"But does he agree with them?" Her eyes moved down his arms and back to his eyes, and Joss got the impression that she was checking him out—against her will. Maybe they had more in common than he thought.

Henry chimed in with an exasperated tone. "Excuse me, I'm still right here and, in case either of you is wondering, my hearing totally works."

"Sorry, Henry." Joss tore his gaze from Kat long enough to cast Henry an apologetic glance. He hadn't meant to push Henry out of the conversation. He was just feeling really conflicted about seeing Kat again after so long. On one hand, he and Kat had grown very close in a short period of time. She'd been there for him through the trials of his initial Slayer training. She'd been a lighthouse to him in many ways. But after Sirus had died, she'd become a threat to his existence.

Joss swallowed hard in realization.

Sirus. Sirus was still alive. Did Kat know? Did she have any idea?

She traced a heart on the back of Henry's right hand with her finger. Her nails were painted in purple glitter polish. "Sorry."

The look on Henry's face said that he forgave her immediately.

"I have to use the restroom." Henry slid out of the booth and pointed a warning finger straight at Joss. "Be careful what you do."

Joss felt his face flush red. Henry might as well

have screamed at him not to make out with Kat while he was gone. As if Joss wanted anything to do with that activity.

Betraying him, Joss's eyes traced a line from Kat's sparkling eyes down her cheekbone to her lips.

No. He didn't want anything to do with Kat in that way. They were once friends, now enemies. Besides, there was a girl in pink who lived in Bathory that Joss couldn't get out of his mind. He had to focus on that girl, not this one. This one wasn't good for him. This one was trouble.

He didn't respond to Henry at all, just dropped his gaze to the table and tried to keep it there. After Henry had gone, Kat gestured to the seat across from her and said, "You might as well sit down."

He stood there stubbornly for a moment, silently debating whether or not sitting in a booth with Kat could be considered fraternizing with the enemy. Once he decided that it was more like reconnaissance than anything, he slid into Henry's seat and looked at her. "What are you doing here exactly, Kat?"

"You know why I'm here, Joss. It's time for me to get revenge for what you took from me. For what you did to Sirus." When she uttered her father's name, the strength that seemed to ebb from her faltered. Her voice shook as she spoke it aloud, evidence of the pain that she must still be feeling. Pain that Joss had never intended to cause.

Without thinking, he reached across the table and cupped her hand in his. To his amazement, she didn't pull away. "Listen, Kat. About Sirus—"

"Help!" A woman burst through the doors into the café, a panicked look in her eye, drawing the attention of every person in the café—even Henry, who'd just then exited the restroom. Her chest was rising and falling in quick breaths, as if she'd been running. "A man needs help! Somebody call an ambulance—a man was just attacked!"

No one in the café moved—no one but Joss, who jumped up from his seat and hurried outside, pushing past the people who were frozen in shock that something violent had just occurred in their vicinity. As he moved out the door, he saw a man in his midtwenties lying on the ground in a pool of blood, his skin paling as the seconds ticked by, his neck bleeding profusely. He was losing blood. A lot of blood. And if someone didn't do something quickly, the man was going to die.

Joss pulled his overshirt off and knelt beside the wounded man, pressing his shirt into the man's neck. Keeping pressure on it might be enough to save him, but not without professional help. He looked at one of the onlookers and made sure the man met his eyes.

Then, calmly but firmly, said, "You. Call an ambulance right now. Tell them this man has had his carotid artery severed and has lost a lot of blood. They need to hurry."

The man nodded and pulled out his cell phone. Once he'd dialed and was actually speaking to someone, Joss relaxed a bit. That was the thing about people in a crisis situation. No one would take responsibility unless you handed it to them.

His overshirt had soaked through, but he kept the pressure on. The man's face was turning white. With one hand keeping pressure on the wound, Joss removed his T-shirt with his other hand, pulling it off over his head. He pressed it into the overshirt as hard as he could without strangling the poor man.

A group of people was gathering and chatter moved like a wave through the crowd, but Joss didn't take any of it in. The woman who'd entered the café had come back outside and was standing beside the man, ringing her hands in worry. Joss met her eyes and spoke calmly. "Did you see who did this?"

"Hard to remember. It's all a blur." She shook her head, looking very much as if she felt she wasn't being much help at all. What she didn't realize was that she'd just told Joss some pretty key information about the attack. She had difficulty remembering the face, which suggested mind control. Which meant that it was a vampire that had attacked this man, further evidenced by the gushing neck wound. Messy, messy, messy.

A man in a tan polo shirt stepped forward and said, "Whatever it was that got him ran down the board-walk and into the woods right after. I saw him. Must have been a psycho or something. Do you think it could be a serial killer?"

Joss didn't bother explaining that in order to be a serial killer, there needed to be a series of similar deaths. In the distance, he heard an ambulance siren. He gestured for the man to kneel beside him and then put the man's hands on the T-shirt in place of his own. "Keep pressure on this. And keep people away from the woods. Where exactly did you see the attacker go?"

"Across the street from the boardwalk entrance, straight into the trees. Be careful, kid. Maybe you should wait for the authorities." The man's eyes wid-ened, and Joss nodded in response. He wasn't about to tell the guy that when it came to vampire attacks, he was one of the authorities.

He hurried away from the scene, down the board-walk. As he moved, the ambulance passed him, and he hoped they'd be able to save the victim. It was only then that it occurred to him that his stake had been exposed to all of the people on the scene. He won-dered if any of them saw it there on his hip, and if they had any idea what it was. Once he reached the end of the boardwalk, he stepped into the woods and slipped his stake from the holster, ready for anything.

He hoped, anyway.

The woods seemed eerily still as he slowly made his way deeper inside. No birds sang songs above him in the trees. No breeze rustled the leaves overhead. No woodland creatures stirred in the undergrowth. It seemed to be just Joss in the woods, nothing more. But he knew that was not true.

Joss scanned the area around him, and as he turned his head to the right, he saw it. That vital piece of evidence that he'd been looking for. That thing that told him that he was on the right path to locating whoever—or whatever—had attacked that man on the boardwalk. On the leaf of a low-growing fern, there on the forest floor, was a single, fresh droplet of blood.

He knelt beside it to get a better look. There was no denying how fresh it was, but he could only guess that it had come from the wounded man. He only hoped that the attacker hadn't been Sirus. But there was only one way to find out. Standing, his fingers gripping his stake, Joss straightened his shoulders and called out, "Sirus? It's Joss."

There was a slight breeze, barely enough to move a few of Joss's hairs out of his eyes. He might not have noticed it, except there had been nothing before it at all, giving weight to the action. Suddenly, a vampire was standing just inches from him, staring him down with a gleam in his eye that suggested that he was hungry, or angry, or both. "A pleasure to make your acquaintance, Joss. But I'm not Sirus."

Joss tried to bring his stake up, but the beast moved with that unbelievable vampire speed again, grabbing Joss by the wrist that held the stake. He shook his head slowly. "You don't want to start anything with me, boy. Trust me."

As quickly as he could move, Joss rolled his wrist to the outside, breaking the vampire's grip. He brought the stake around, aiming for its chest, but as he did so, the vampire swore. It shoved Joss hard, sending him flying. A moment later, Joss struck a tree's trunk with his back. When he hit, his lungs seized momentarily, knocking the wind from him. At the same time, his hand opened, releasing the stake. It fell to the ground, but Joss had no idea where. As his body collapsed to the forest floor, he searched, but it was gone. He was unarmed and completely unsure of how he was going to get out of this situation.

The nameless vampire jumped, coming at him, but Joss rolled to his right before springing to his feet. As he did, he turned and brought his foot up, roundhouse kicking the creature in the side. The force of his kick sent the surprised vampire into a nearby tree. Thinking quickly, Joss grabbed it by the shoulder and threw it into another tree.

Only the vampire was thinking quicker.

With surprising grace, it planted its feet on the tree trunk and ran up the side of the tree before flipping over and landing behind Joss. As Joss turned to face it, the creature caught him with a right hook. As its fist met with Joss's cheek, it felt like his head had exploded. Pain vibrated through his skull. But he wasn't going to let pain stand in his way.

Joss spun around, backhanding the beast. As it stumbled, Joss caught it in the ribs with his knee. The vampire tumbled to the ground, where Joss kicked it hard in the side. Angrily, it shouted up at him, "Stop, Joss! You don't know what you're doing!"

Miraculously, his stake was lying right beside the vampire. Joss grabbed it and raised it in the air as quickly as he could. "For you, Cecile."

He planted his stake hard in the vampire's chest. The vampire screamed, clutching at the wood, his eyes full of disbelief. Then, as the light was leaving its eyes, it said, "Be careful, little Slayer. I'm not the worst thing in these woods."

Joss sat back, panting from their fight. He was about to ask the vampire what it had meant, when he realized that it was dead. He looked around the woods, with the question instead in his eyes.

· 10 ·

CAUGHT IN THE ACT

Joss had no idea how he was supposed to request a cleanup without a cell phone, but it was probably a good idea that he stop by Paty's house on the way home to report in. He was hoping that maybe Paty had a shirt he could wear as well, and that maybe she wouldn't mind if he took a shower there. As Joss freed his stake from the vampire's corpse, he heard a sound. Spinning around, he was ready for anything. But what he saw was his cousin Henry, standing there staring at him in disbelief and horror. Not two steps behind him was Kat, looking just a little bit smug and a little bit sad.

Joss had no idea what to say. He couldn't explain the vampire's death any more than he could explain why he was holding the stake. And he certainly hadn't wanted his cousin to see him like this. It was one thing for Henry to know that Joss was a Slayer. It was a quite another for him to see Joss in action, or at least in the immediate aftermath of a takedown.

Henry stepped forward and looked from Joss to the vampire and back. At first, Joss thought he was going to say something about what a horrible thing it was that Joss had done, or that maybe he'd ask Joss if the vampire had attacked him. But Henry reacted in a way that, for whatever reason, Joss hadn't been expecting.

Without a word, Henry drew his arm back and punched Joss in the gut. Hard. It hurt, but Joss's Slayer instincts were stronger than pain. Before he knew it, he had Henry by the wrist, twisted around, and pinned with his face against a tree. Kat beat at his back, screaming, "Stop it! You'll break his arm, Joss!"

With a shaking breath, Joss released his cousin and stepped back in utter shock at his own actions. He hadn't meant to grab Henry like that. Who knows what he might have done if Kat hadn't stopped him?

"Henry, are you okay? Did he hurt you?" Kat looked over Henry's wrist with obvious upset. She glared at Joss and tried to gently coax Henry away. "Come on. We need to get that checked out right away. It might be broken. I can't believe you call that guy your friend. Family's one thing, but who does that to a friend?"

Henry cradled his wrist in his hand, his fingers paling and shaking slightly. Joss wondered if it really was broken. Henry shouted back to Joss, who was standing beside the vampire's corpse in a daze. "You're a monster, Joss! You know that?"

And Joss did. He did know that. He was a monster.

But at least the people of Santa Carla were safe now.

The last thing Henry said to him before disappearing with Kat was softer spoken, but still immeasurably angry. "I can't believe you did this."

Joss couldn't help but feel like Kat had gotten what she wanted for the moment. With a deep sigh, he looked slowly around at the forest that surrounded him, slipping his stake back into the leather holster on his hip with complete disregard of the blood that was still coating its surface. One thought played on repeat in his mind: The thing about monsters is that there's always something worse out there.

· 11 ·

CURIOSITY AND THE CAT

Joss stood still with his thoughts, going over in his mind what had just transpired, for several minutes after doing what he could to hide the vampire's remains until a Slayer Society cleanup crew could step in and take care of things. He'd covered the body with fallen leaves, fallen branches, and hoped that no human would find it. Death wasn't something that humans typically dealt well with. It also wasn't, Joss thought, something that Slayers dealt with either. The distinction in his mind between human and Slayer had come suddenly, but it seemed to fit. He didn't feel like a human half the time. He felt like something that operated on the fringe of humanity.

He moved through the woods for almost a half mile before exiting, not wanting anyone who had been at the boardwalk to see him and wonder why he was spattered with fresh blood and who that blood might belong to. He didn't go home. Too many questions were waiting for him there. Questions that his parents might ask about why he was shirtless and bloody. Questions that Henry might ask about why Joss would do something like that to his cousin, to his blood brother.

Blood. There was too much blood in Joss's life.

Still dazed by what had just happened, Joss found himself standing in front of Paty's small cottage. After all, she was supposed to be there for him—and if all that meant was that she'd loan him her shower and maybe a fresh shirt, that was enough. It was all Joss needed at the moment. And what he definitely didn't need were questions.

He raised his fist to rap on the door, but before he could speak a word, Paty called from within, her voice soft and ragged, as if she'd been crying. "It's open, Joss. Come on in."

As he turned the knob and pushed, he leaned in and saw her face. Her eyes were red, her cheeks blotched. Paty had been crying. It was a strange thing to see. Paty didn't cry. She was tough. What could break someone like her? He stepped inside, closing the door behind him. "Everything okay?"

Her brows came together as she gave him a once-over. As she spoke, she moved toward him, her eyes full of concern. "Seems like I should be the one asking that. What happened? Are you hurt?"

Joss shook his head and held a hand up, stopping her approach. With the other hand, he gestured to the burgundy flakes that had dried all over his chest and stomach. "It's not as bad as it looks. Hardly any of it is my blood."

Paty paused midstep, folded her arms in front of her, and raised an eyebrow. Her eyes were no longer red, her tears moving so quickly into the past that Joss began to wonder whether or not he had imagined them. "Tell me what isn't yours belongs to that little weenie that runs the comic book shop."

A smirk tugged at the corner of his mouth. Apparently he wasn't the only one who didn't care for Edgar Frog. "No such luck. I stumbled on a vampire attack and took care of business. I did my best to hide the body, but I need a cleanup. Redwood State Park. East side, about a hundred yards in."

"On it." Paty grabbed her phone off the counter and hit number two on speed dial. After giving directions to the mysterious voice on the other end, she hit End and turned back to Joss. "Do you think this vampire might be the one responsible for the recent deaths?"

Truth be told, Joss didn't want to think much about his Slayer responsibilities at the moment. What he really wanted was to take a hot shower, put on a clean shirt, and then maybe rewind a few years, back to when he and Henry were friends and brothers. But he knew that that would never happen. Time only ever marched forward, no matter how hard you pushed back.

"Not really. I have an idea who . . ." He bit the inside of his cheek for a moment, hoping that Paty either wouldn't notice that he'd just referred to a vampire as a person rather than a thing. His uncle Abraham would have punished him for a slipup like that for sure. ". . . *what* might be responsible, but I don't know how to say it. Between you and me, Paty, I don't really want to say it at all."

The last sentence came out in a whisper, and when it did, Joss's heart reached out after it, but only managed to grab air. He knew better than to say things like that. He knew better than to ever admit to anything at all like that. Especially to another Slayer. The punishment of withholding information from a fellow member of the Society could be severe.

But this wasn't just any member of the Society,

he told himself. This was Paty. If he could trust any member of his team, it was her.

She tilted her head to the side curiously. "Who?"

There was that word again. Who. This time Paty had said it. Which might mean that they were both sharing the same questions about whether vampires were people or things. Or maybe he was just reading too much into it . . . which was likely the case.

Joss wet his lips and met Paty's eyes, hoping that she wouldn't freak out the way that he'd felt like freaking out when he'd found out that Sirus was still alive. After taking a slow, deep breath, he released it in words that felt almost too intense to be spoken aloud. They were life-changing words. And Joss didn't feel important enough to be changing anyone's life. "I think . . . that maybe Sirus is the vampire responsible for the deaths. Paty . . . he didn't die in that explosion. I just saw him the other day. Sirus is still alive."

To Joss's shock, Paty didn't even flinch at the news. Instead, she said, "You probably want to grab a shower, right? I think I have one of Morgan's T-shirts around here somewhere that you can borrow."

"Paty." He shook his head at her, confounded. What? Was she in denial? Did she think that he was kidding? Joss would never kid about something like that. This was supposed to be life-changing news. Why was she acting like it wasn't really news at all?

"Didn't you hear me? I said that Sirus is still alive."

"I heard you, Joss. But . . . well . . . you're not exactly telling me anything that I didn't already know." She sighed as Joss stood there, shaking his head still, trying to wrap his mind around what it was that she was saying. Then she nodded toward the bathroom door. "Take your shower. Then we'll talk. Towels are in the cabinet over the sink. I'll find you a shirt."

He stood there for a moment, not knowing exactly what he was supposed to say to her and struggling with the growing realization that Paty hadn't been surprised. She'd known about Sirus. Which made him wonder what else she knew that she wasn't sharing with him.

Without another word, he moved down the short hall to the small bathroom. The towels were right where she'd told him they'd be, and when he stripped down and stepped into the shower, the hot water felt good on his skin. As he watched the blood run down the drain, Joss thought about the movies. In movies, killing wasn't all that messy. Blood hardly went anywhere. The mess of it was easy to contain. But the reality, he'd found, was far different. Blood got everywhere, and it refused to be easily cleansed away. Plus, it smelled. It took a lot of soap just to remove the rotten, metallic scent from his skin, and even then, he knew he wouldn't feel completely clean for the next few days. It was as if the essence of the blood clung to him, the memory of the horrific act that he'd performed.

He didn't know what was going on with Paty, or how she'd known anything about Sirus still being alive. But he did know that he trusted her. And if she had good reason not to tell him about Sirus, reason beyond the fact that he was supposed to be on his own this summer, then it was okay. She'd explain everything, and then maybe Joss could go back to not feeling betrayed.

Because he felt that way. And it hurt.

Once his skin and hair were clean, Joss stepped out of the shower, toweled dry, and got dressed again. He dropped his towel, now tinged from the blood that had refused to be rinsed away, in the hamper and stepped out into the hall. Paty was in the kitchen. As she tossed him a clean T-shirt, the timer on the oven went off. Donning a bright pink oven mitt, she opened the oven door and pulled out a tray of freshly baked snickerdoodle cookies.

Joss sat wordlessly on one of the bar stools by the kitchen island, his eyes on the pan that she was placing on the stove. Cookies. Clearly, he was either in trouble or in for some bad news. He had to be. She'd felt the need to soften the blow with cinnamon and sugar deliciousness.

Paty slid two hot cookies onto a plate with the aid of a spatula and set it in front of Joss. He grabbed one immediately and bit into it, breathing out a series of sounds that weren't really words, but somehow helped to cool his burning mouth. "Hawthawthawthawthawt!"

She poured a glass of cool milk, and Joss couldn't drink it fast enough. After he emptied it, his stomach gurgled a little, but at least his mouth felt better. He left the second cookie on the plate, giving it time to cool, and looked at Paty. "So you knew. About Sirus surviving that explosion."

"Yes." She removed her oven mitt, tossing it casually on the counter. Then she turned back to Joss, a newly born tension in her stance. "I knew."

"How long have you known? Since the beginning? And you never told me? I've been living with crushing guilt for two years and you just let me live with it? You let me believe that I killed my mentor? My friend? Kat's dad?" He hadn't intended to raise his voice or to stand, his chest heaving in anger, but that's just what he did. It wasn't right for Paty to have kept this from him. Sirus had been a beacon of comfort for him during an incredibly difficult time. He'd been there for Joss when it seemed that no other Slayer would help him. More than that, he'd been like a father to Joss. His betrayal had stung, but what had stung far worse was the false knowledge that Joss had been responsible for Sirus's death.

"Hold it right there." Paty pointed at him with a lone finger, and then gestured for him to take his seat again. Out of respect, he did. Then it was Paty's turn to raise her voice. "First and foremost, I hadn't known from the beginning. I only learned of his survival this spring, and didn't tell you because I was under strict orders by the Society not to. What with your loyalty under question and whatnot. Loyalty—you know— that thing that the Slayer Society values more than anything. That thing that you've been apparently lacking ever since the day you met that Vlad kid."

Joss winced. He couldn't refute what she was saying. It was true. It was all true. He hadn't been nearly as loyal in thought or in deed as the Slayer Society required or deserved. But he couldn't blame Vlad for that, or even Paty for pointing it out. He could only blame himself.

"Second, don't forget that that friend and mentor of yours was also a *vampire*."

The word hung in the air between them for a moment. It felt heavy. It felt wrong. And what was worse was that the truth of that word felt so much heavier than the word itself.

Joss hated that Sirus was a vampire. He hated that he still cared about Sirus. He hated that he still cared about Vlad. But he was beginning to think that that aspect of him could never be changed. What if everyone he came to care about betrayed him in some way? Sirus, Dorian, Vlad—it seemed that he was meant to be more of a vampire's plaything than a Slayer. The very idea sent a bitter shiver up his spine. Chasing it was the whisper of sorrow.

The look on Paty's face said that she felt very much the same way that Joss did. It made Joss wonder how the Slayer Society felt about Paty and her loyalties to them. They questioned his loyalty. Why not question hers?

"He betrayed us, Joss. Not just the Society. He betrayed our team, and did so over a long course of time. Plus, he wasn't just your friend. He was also mine. So don't think that you're the only one affected by his perceived death or surprising survival."

Joss released a quiet sigh. What Paty was forgetting was that she didn't exactly have to carry the weight of guilt at having been the person who'd caused Sirus's perceived death.

Paty braced herself with her hands on the countertop and hung her head for a moment—long enough to take two or three really slow, deep breaths, as if she needed to gather her wits before she spoke again. Then she met Joss's eyes, and when she spoke again, he realized that he'd been behaving rather selfishly. He wasn't alone in this pain, in this confusion. She shared it. "I'm freaked out, too, y'know."

Joss eyed his remaining cookie for a moment, but had no desire whatsoever to pick it up and continue eating. Suddenly his mouth tasted sour, unworthy of a sugary reward. He met Paty's eyes with an apology. "I'm sorry. I shouldn't bite your head off just for following Society orders. I just . . . it was a surprise to see him."

She nodded slowly, and it was clear to Joss by the look in her eyes that she was mourning the loss of her friendship with Sirus still. "How is he?"

"He looked fine. Healthy, I think. But worried. He said there's something in the woods." There was. There was something in the woods. Joss just wasn't sure whether or not that thing was Sirus or something else.

Paty folded her arms across her chest and tilted her head to the side in contemplation. "It could be a trick. Something to distract from him."

Joss nodded. His thoughts exactly. "It could be. I need to look at the coroner's report for Tilly, the woman who lived near the café, just to confirm that she was killed by a vampire and not . . . something else. How can I get my hands on it? I mean, the coroner isn't likely to just hand something like that over to a random teenager."

Paty tore her gaze away from him then and rubbed her hands on her arms, as if trying to warm them against a nonexistent chill in the air. It took her a moment to speak again, and when she did, she seemed extremely uncomfortable. "I can't help you, Joss. No one can."

She flicked her eyes to him momentarily, but then her gaze was gone again. Joss released a deep sigh, picked up his remaining cookie, and headed for the front door. As he opened it, he nodded to her over his left shoulder. "Okay. Then I'll help myself."

It was a huge relief to Joss that Santa Carla wasn't a really big town and that he was in good shape, because if he'd required a car to reach the coroner's office on the other side of town, he might not have made it to the unassuming building that housed it. He was glad that Henry wasn't tagging along, because there was no way his cousin would go along with breaking and entering—especially in the name of the Slayer Society. Not to mention the countless questions that Henry would ask if Joss lied about their destination. But mostly, he was glad that Henry wasn't with him because Joss was relatively certain that if he got caught, his dad was going to skin him alive.

The office was winding down business for the day, and for several minutes, Joss stood outside on the sidewalk next to a bus stop, looking expectantly down the street, hoping that no one would give him a second glance. After all, who suspected anything criminal from a clean-cut teenager waiting for the bus? He'd learned from his online research that a person had to be eighteen years of age to request medical records or a coroner's report, and since Joss wasn't yet that old, he was going to have to get creative.

The office closed at 5:00 P.M. And that's when his creativity would kick in.

A police officer passed by on the sidewalk and nodded a hello to Joss, who smiled in return and went back to pretending that he was waiting for an overdue bus. After a while, no one else exited the building, and Joss couldn't see any lights on inside. He glanced around casually to make sure he was in the clear. Once he was certain he was alone, Joss slipped around the side of the building, under the cover of several large bushes that obstructed the view of any passersby. He walked along the brick wall until he spied his golden opportunity—a window fan that had been left wedged in an open window. It had been warm lately in Santa Carla, and apparently the person in that office had thought that a window fan was a wise move. Joss imagined their boss would be furious if they found out. But he wasn't here to teach anyone a lesson. He had to get in, get a glimpse at Tilly's coroner's report, and get out.

The great thing about old buildings is that they're generally built to be sturdy, and architects who appreciated sturdiness also appreciated large windowsills. Joss jumped up, gripping his fingers on the windowsill by the fan, and pulled himself up, until he was perched outside the window of one of the first floor offices. Holding his breath and hoping that the open window meant that this office didn't have an alarm at the ready, Joss gently pushed the window open. When no alarm sounded, he breathed a quiet sigh of relief and set the window fan inside on the floor before climbing in after it.

The office itself was boring and plain. Steel desks, too many stacks of papers, and big, gray filing cabinets lining the walls. After looking around for a bit, Joss realized that he was in the wrong place entirely. As quietly as possible, even though he was relatively certain that the building was empty, Joss moved out into the hall and checked a small directory hanging on the wall. The sheriff's office was on the third floor, so he could only hope that the coroner's office was as well. He climbed the stairs quickly and when he reached the third floor, he was greeted by a small green placard next to the door that read CORONER'S OFFICE.

He tried the knob, but someone had remembered to lock the door when they left, so Joss reached into his backpack and cursed under his breath. His lock

pick set was sitting at home on his nightstand—
forgotten there after its recent thorough cleaning.
Picking a lock without the right tools wasn't impossible, but it sure as hell wasn't easy. What he really
needed was a hairpin, and maybe an Allen wrench.
Moving down the hall, he tried a few doors, but each
was locked, so he made his way back down the stairs
to the office he'd entered the building from. Sitting
on the desk there was the only thing close enough to
a lock pick that was going to get Joss inside the coroner's office, so he grabbed it and headed back upstairs,
cursing in his mind the entire way.

There's something jarring about the sound of
broken glass, and as Joss smashed the small window
with the heavy paperweight he'd found two things
happened: One, he hoped like hell that he was right
about the building being empty, and two, he turned
his head to the side and squeezed his eyes shut, fear-
ing that a splinter of glass might fly out and cut him,
despite the fact that the window of that particular door
was made of tempered glass. The moment the paperweight made contact, the entire window cracked in a
zillion tiny zigzag lines before crumbling to pieces all
over the floor. It was a messy job, but Joss thought
it was probably better to do a smash and grab and
get out of the building as quickly as possible, rather

than take his time performing a seamless, undetectable entry. He was quite certain, however, that his uncle Abraham would disagree.

He pushed open the door and, after just a few minutes, located the cabinets holding the files of the recently deceased. Luckily, the files were kept in pristine alphabetical order, so it wasn't long before Joss had Tilly's file in his hands and was poring over its contents. Most of what the coroner had to say about Tilly's death had been expected, but one small note gave him pause. Pause enough to realize that maybe the Slayer Society did know what they were talking about, and that maybe it really was a vampire that was responsible for the recent deaths in Santa Carla.

Deceased showed signs of acute, severe anemia.

Anemia. Which meant the lack of red blood cells. Which was exactly what happened when a vampire drained a person.

Joss returned the file to the cabinet and headed back downstairs, his thoughts heavy. If the vampire that he'd killed in the woods wasn't the one responsible for the recent deaths, and he'd seen no evidence that had suggested another vampire was in the area, then it had to be Sirus. This meant that Sirus was lying to him . . . again. And it meant something else, too. It meant that he was going to have to take Sirus down. He was going to have to kill his friend all over again. What was it that people often said about history repeating itself?

As Joss dropped outside of the open window that had been holding that fan, a voice greeted him, startling him some. But it wasn't a voice that he knew. As he turned around to face the speaker, he realized that he was dead the moment he saw his dad again. Standing there before him was the cop that he'd seen earlier out at the bus stop. With his hand on the gun on his hip, the officer said, "I'm betting you don't have any business being in there, now do you, son?"

Fear sent a chill through Joss's limbs. He held his hands out to the side, so that the officer wouldn't think he was trying to resist at all. "No, sir. But then again, I've never been a betting man."

Joss smiled, hoping that a bit of humor might help him get off with a warning. When the officer didn't smile back, he thought that a different approach might be better. "I'm sorry, sir. I was just curious."

As the cop gripped Joss's arm and led Joss away from the building, he said, "Curiosity killed the cat, son. You should be more careful not to be so curious. Come on. Let's get you home."

Joss had never been in the back of a police car before, and the moment he was, he hoped that he'd never be there again. There was something about knowing that he couldn't escape, that he was at the mercy of the officer that sent a sick feeling through his stomach. Or maybe that was just because he knew that once he got home, he was dead.

The officer put the car in gear, and after a few moments of silence, he said, "You want to tell me what you were looking for in there? The sheriff's office isn't exactly a place for teenagers. No drugs in there."

"I don't do drugs." Joss's words cut off the officer's last spoken syllable. Joss didn't do drugs, had never done drugs, would never do drugs. He didn't need a foreign substance to get a rush. His daily existence gave him all the rush he could handle. He didn't need to poison his body. Clarity was key when it came to slaying vampires.

"That's good. Drugs will mess up your life." The officer glanced at Joss in the rearview mirror. His eyes were sharp blue. "So what was it?"

Joss could have lied. But he was tired of lying. Besides, something in the officer's eyes said that if Joss lied, he'd know, somehow. So Joss went with the truth—no matter how strange it felt to do so. Shrugging, he said, "I heard about the death of this woman named Tilly by gardening shears, and I wanted to know if the coroner knew anything that the papers didn't."

In the mirror, Joss saw the officer frown. After a

moment, he said, "I knew Tilly. Nice lady. Her death was pretty shocking. But trust me, kid. There's nothing else to know. Certainly nothing else to warrant a boy your age breaking into the coroner's office."

Joss disagreed, but he didn't offer up that bit of information. "I'm sorry."

"Sorry you did it, or sorry you got caught?" The officer met his eyes again, and this time, the crinkles by his eyes suggested a smile on his lips.

"Honestly?" Honest. The way non-Slayers had the freedom to be all the time. "That second one."

"Promise me you'll stick to the library the next time you get curious."

Joss shook his head. It wasn't that he wanted to be a lawbreaker. It's just that sometimes, in order to do his duty as a Slayer, he was forced to ignore the laws of mankind. "I'm afraid I can't do that, sir."

"Well, then at least promise me that you'll stay away from the coroner's office. Next time I catch you, it'll be handcuffs and paperwork."

Outside the window was a blur of green as they passed trees and grass and greenery. Joss bet that if they slowed down a bit, it would be really beautiful scenery. Life was like that, he imagined. If he could just slow down, maybe he could see the beauty in things.

"Okay." He met the cop's reflection again. "I promise."

"Where do you live, exactly?"

Joss was tempted not to tell him. Prison might be a better option than facing his dad's wrath. But eventually, he told the officer where he lived, and after what felt like a long car ride, they pulled into the driveway, where Joss's dad looked up from the woodpile with surprise, fear, and then fury. Joss sank down in his seat, watching as the officer got out and spoke with his dad, kicking himself for not thinking to lie and give the policeman Paty's address instead.

Then he came back to the car, opened Joss's door. "No more trouble, son. You hear me? Next time, this will be serious."

Only it was already serious.

Joss was in very real trouble with his dad, and he wasn't exactly sure how to face it. As the cop pulled away, he turned back to his dad and tried. "Dad, I'm sorry. I was ju—"

"Don't talk to me. I don't want to hear it." He shook his head, his eyes burning with anger.

Joss understood that. He did. Who wouldn't be angry at their kid for coming home in the back of a cop car? It was a perfectly sensible reaction. But he hadn't even given Joss a chance to explain.

Not that Joss had really taken the time to come up with a believable explanation. The truth wasn't an option here. "But Dad, I—"

He tossed another log on the woodpile, but did it with such force that he might have been tossing it more *at* the pile than *on* it. "First you attack Henry and now you get brought home by the police? What's *wrong* with you, Joss?"

More than he would ever know. Joss was a liar. He was a secret keeper. He was a killer. But all for the right reasons . . . or so he thought. What if the reasons that he'd deemed to be right were actually wrong? Then he was just a liar, a secret keeper, and a killer, without good cause. Then he was just a terrible person.

Joss shrugged, shoving his thumbs in his front jeans pockets. "A lot, I guess."

"You guess." His dad snorted then and tossed another hunk of wood onto the pile before turning back to Joss and pointing an accusing finger at him. "You're damn right, a lot. Why can't you be more like Greg or Henry? They'd never be so reckless."

Joss stood there, stunned. What was he supposed to say to that? How was he supposed to respond to the admission that his dad wished that he were someone else, rather than his reckless, imperfect self?

Fighting tears, Joss turned toward the house and hurried away. He could only leave his dad with the words that he feared most. "You're right."

Echoing after him were his father's angry words.

"Don't you walk away from me when I'm talking to you!"

As Joss stepped inside the side door, he passed by Henry, whose wrist was in a brace. With his uninjured hand, Henry squeezed Joss's shoulder sympathetically, but Joss shook him off and hurried upstairs. He wasn't sure where this unexpected bout of empathy had come from, but it was a case of too little, too late. He didn't want Henry's sympathy. He didn't want his father's approval. All he really wanted at the moment was to be left alone.

· 12 ·

WORKING IT OUT

J oss ran as hard and fast as he could, straight at the pole that held the ratty-looking tetherball. As he jumped, he focused hard on the way that his muscles felt, on the speed that he knew he was capable of. He focused, true enough, on anything that wasn't his dad or Henry or his home life or anything at all like that. He focused only on what he could control, and that was this. The way his body moved. The shape his physical form was in. Because focusing on his emotional form was the last thing that Joss wanted. Physical stuff was easy. Emotional . . . not so much.

He'd snuck out of the house to come here, to

gain some perspective on things and to run through some maneuvers. But if his dad found out, he was as good as dead. He was amazed that his dad had let him walk into the house without strangling him, but the grounding that had come after his dad had entered was no surprise at all. Not that it mattered. How can you ground a Slayer?

He jumped high, planting his left foot on the pole and pushed off, launching himself toward the swing set. As he flew through the air, he focused on the landing that he wanted to achieve, repeating three words in his brain: *Visualize and realize.*

His right hand closed around the metal of the slanted pole of the swing set. Kicking his legs at just the right angle, it provided him with just enough momentum to make a full circle around the pole. When he was again under the A-frame support, he grabbed the other pole in his left hand. Joss alternated hands climbing closer to the top of the frame. Right, left. Right, left.

Once there, he reached out for the large crossbeam at the top of the swings. This pole was much bigger than the side supports. His palms wet with sweat, Joss found it much more difficult to maintain his grip, but he held fast, pushing his efforts onward. He pulled himself up, bending over the beam at the waist. Then he swung one leg over the bar and stood nimbly on the top of it.

Running forward, one foot directly in front of the other, he worked his way ever closer to the end of the swing set. At the last second, Joss jumped off the beam, grabbed a tree branch, and swung forward, landing with his feet directly on the top of a long, metal slide. With the kind of finesse possessed by only Slayers, he glided effortlessly to the bottom, coming to rest still standing in the sand below.

He quickly squashed his urge to pat himself on the back for doing a good job at his various training exercises. After all, he didn't deserve congratulations or admiration for running through basic maneuvers. He didn't deserve such an arrogant show of self-flattery. He'd done nothing. Nothing but fail.

For only the briefest of moments, Joss paused to catch his breath. His muscles were burning. His forehead dripping with sweat. A strange pain was gnawing at his right side, just beneath the ribs. But all that Joss could think about was Sirus, and how he'd failed both the Society and Sirus by not killing the vampire the moment that he encountered him here in Santa Carla. Not to mention that he had also failed himself.

If he had killed Sirus at that moment, it would have pleased the Society to know that he fully understood his job as a Slayer. It would have proven his loyalty to them. It would have made them believe in him once again.

Killing Sirus would have been an act of kindness, really. What person, what Slayer, would really want to live the life of a vampire? What if Sirus was suffering in this form? What if he was trapped? Joss might have set him free with one swipe of a stake.

It would have been the right thing to do. So why did the idea of doing it make Joss feel queasy?

Maybe he was losing his edge. Maybe the Slayer Society was right to be concerned. He could run as many maneuvers and training exercises as he wanted around this old, abandoned playground. None of it mattered. What mattered was that he had failed to kill Sirus that summer, and he had failed again this summer. He was a failure. He was weak.

And he wasn't at all sure that he cared.

So what if he was weak? So what if he was feeling more than a little conflicted over vampires and their place in this world? Was he really the only one, the first of his kind, the sole Slayer, to wonder whether or not all vampires were truly evil? And if he was, was being the first to wonder really such a horrible thing?

Sirus had been like a father figure to him. And Vlad . . . Vlad had been his friend. The truth was, when no one else was around and Joss was left alone with his thoughts, he treasured the time that he'd spent with each of them. And he immediately felt guilty for doing so. Were these thoughts, these emotions, wrong simply because the Slayer Society said that they were? Or was it even the smallest bit possible that it was okay to feel positive emotions about a sworn enemy?

He wondered if the Society was right about vampires being able to trick your emotional reaction to situations. Had Sirus and Vlad hit switches in his brain, causing him to feel this way? Or was it how he really felt?

Joss shook his head and started running laps around the playground, trying to clear his tormented thoughts away. He didn't want to think about Sirus and Vlad anymore. He just wanted all that he had been through to fall away and crumble into the dust of his memories.

But as his feet slowed, and Joss wiped salty sweat and tears from his eyes, he saw the truth of it. There was no going back. He'd been set on a path of discovery, and he had to face it head on if he had any hope at all of understanding what was right and what was wrong. He'd taken an oath—a promise—to the Slayer Society that he would do all that he could for the good of mankind. And if that meant losing a friend, if it meant losing a father figure, then that was the way that it had to be.

A father figure.

Joss blinked with sudden, sad, angry realization. By the time he'd met Sirus, Sirus had already been turned into a vampire. Therefore, Sirus already had vampire motivations. What if Sirus had honed in on Joss's desperate need for a father figure in his life from the moment that they'd met, and had just been using that need to get Joss to give him what he wanted? What if Sirus's apparent affection for him had been nothing but a mirage? A tool to manipulate a young, inexperienced Slayer into doing his bidding? What if that's what Sirus was doing now, and that's why Joss had stayed his hand and failed to kill Sirus when he saw him in the woods? What if Sirus had been controlling Joss's emotions with his mind?

Joss balled his fists tightly at his sides. If that were true, then it would mean that Sirus was the killer after all. If that were true, it would mean that Joss had been nothing but a pawn in a bloodsucking monster's twisted game.

The sun dipped down below the trees then, turning the sky above a fiery shade of orange. Joss retrieved his T-shirt from where it lay on the rusted merry-go-round and as he slipped it over his head, he hoped that Sirus's telepathy was honing in on him. As hard as he could, he thought about his former friend and mentor and hoped that Sirus would hear his thoughts and listen. His message, as he stepped from the playground and into the surrounding woods, was short, but clear. *"Sirus . . . we need to talk."*

As he lifted his left foot from the grass of the playground area, Joss moved into the woods. His hand found the comfort of his stake in its holster. It was time for honesty. It was time for truth. It was time for him and Sirus to have a little chat about motives.

And only one of them would get out of the woods alive.

· 13 ·

A CONVERSATION WITH SIRUS

I t amazed Joss how stepping from an open, grassy area and into the edge of a forest could affect the light so drastically. It was almost like moving between worlds. In one, there was the soft glow of a between time, where everything was bathed in the warm tones of sunset. But on the other side of that wall of trees there was darkness. Little light filtered in. Shadows of the towering tree trunks blended in with the undergrowth. Wind moved branches, creating strange woodland demons in Joss's imagination. It was difficult to tell the difference between myth and reality. In the forest, it was night. Night. The realm of vampires.

Joss wasn't certain that what he was doing—wandering into the woods, hoping that Sirus had somehow honed in on his thoughts at that precise moment and heeded his call—wasn't the dumbest thing that he had ever done. But what did it hurt to try to reach Sirus with his thoughts? So what if he came out on the other side looking stupid? He'd only look stupid to himself, and to Joss, it was worth that risk. Especially if he made contact with Sirus and they could settle this all at last.

The blue tint that pervaded the forest gave way to gray, then black, as night fell hard and fast. It was difficult to see in the darkness of the woods, but Joss relaxed his eyes, and allowed them to adjust to the change in light as he surveyed his surroundings for any sign of Sirus. In the distance, he could hear the faint song of frogs, calling to future mates. Not ten yards to his left, there was the sound of some creature crawling through the undergrowth. Standing with his back to a thick-trunked tree, his stake firmly grasped in his right hand, the Slayer Joss McMillan laid in wait.

"About what, Joss? What do we need to talk about?" The voice came from behind him, but there had been no sounds preceding it, as if Sirus hadn't moved at all to get here. He wasn't there, and then he was. Joss couldn't help but marvel at a vampire's unnatural speed.

Joss spun around and found Sirus standing on the other side of the tree, in the exact position that Joss had been standing just a moment before. His face looked drawn, troubled. His posture suggested that he was weary. But it might have been an act. Vampires were tricky that way. Especially this vampire.

"Shall we discuss your nightmares? The murders that have been happening around Santa Carla? The weather?" Sirus met his eyes then, and Joss could tell that Sirus knew exactly why Joss had called him here tonight. As if on cue, Sirus's eyes moved to the stake in Joss's hand. "What else is there for a vampire and a Slayer to discuss?"

Joss didn't move, but he did tighten his grip on his stake a bit, on the chance that Sirus might make an unexpected move toward him. "First, we can discuss the murders, if you like."

Sirus raised an eyebrow then, but not in any way that suggested that Joss didn't know what he was talking about. Just, perhaps, that Joss had only barely scratched the surface of his theories when it came to the murders and who . . . or what . . . might have committed them. "It'll be a short conversation, Joss. I'm afraid I don't have much to offer on the subject. And what I do know about them you wouldn't believe. Not even if I swore on Kat's life."

Hearing him say that gave Joss brief pause. Sirus would never swear on Kat's life. She was his daughter. She was his everything. But he didn't give voice to his doubts, simply tilted his head at his former mentor and friend and tightened his jaw a bit. "Try me."

Sirus nodded to the stake in Joss's hand. "You don't need that."

But he did need his stake. Just in case Sirus lunged at him. He needed it to protect himself, to defend himself from the murderous rampage of a bloodthirsty monster.

Didn't he?

"I'll be the judge of that." Suddenly the stake felt very heavy in his hand. But he gripped it anyway. "Were you and another vampire working in tandem to take innocent lives around Santa Carla?"

Sirus shook his head, meeting Joss's eyes. But Joss could tell that the vampire's focus was still on his stake. "No. But I know the gentleman to whom you are referring. I simply brought him along to assist me in my search for the killer. But you made fast work of him, didn't you? Did it occur to you that his actions toward you might only have been in self-defense and out of fear?"

No. Sirus was wrong. That vampire had been trying to kill him.

"You're right on one thing, though." Sirus continued. "It is a vampire that's responsible for these deaths. But not a normal vampire. Something else. Something . . . monstrous."

Joss met Sirus's eyes, an angry heat rising up his neck and enveloping his face. "You're monstrous."

Sirus held his hands out in front of him in a pleading gesture. When he spoke, his tone was soft, gentle, as if he wanted to do his best to protect Joss from whatever it was that Joss was thinking about doing. "No, Joss. Fangs or not, I am your friend."

The last word that Sirus spoke echoed through Joss's skull like the lie that it was. Who was Sirus kidding? He wasn't Joss's friend. He was the enemy, a monster, someone who'd used Joss's weakness to get what he'd wanted. A friend didn't lie to you. A friend didn't manipulate you. Besides, he'd danced this dance of betrayal before. With a boy named Vladimir Tod.

With fury building up in his chest, Joss made his move. He shot straight for Sirus, raising his stake high, his words spilling out like fire from his tongue. "Like hell you are!"

Sirus grabbed him by the wrist and held Joss's weapon still. His eyes had lit up with something mimicking anger, but his words came out sounding more like regret. "I am, Joss! I know you don't believe it, but I am your friend."

They each struggled for control of the stake, but just as Joss was certain he had the upper hand, Sirus slipped the wooden weapon from his grip and tossed it several feet behind him. After he did, Joss shoved uselessly, angrily at his chest. "You betrayed me, you son of a—"

"Joss!" Sirus shook his head, his eyes rimmed in red and shimmering. "I had no choice. I promise you that. If there had been another way . . . if there had been any other way, Joss . . ."

"You made me think you cared about me. But you were using me. All along. Every moment. Every exchange. Why?" He wasn't shouting anymore, and he was no longer certain that he'd really intended to kill Sirus here in the woods. He'd just wanted answers. He'd just wanted to understand.

Sirus ran a frustrated hand through his hair, raking it back from his face. The sight of his upset put a hard rock at the center of Joss's core. "I didn't want to use you, Joss. I truly care about you. You're . . . you're like a son to me."

Sirus's words tugged at Joss's being, threatening to rip apart any resolve that remained. All Joss had ever wanted was for his dad to love him, and to be the way that he'd been before a vampire had stolen Cecile away from them forever, smashing their family apart as it exited their home. All he'd wanted was to know that he still had a dad, somehow. But Sirus couldn't be his dad. Because flawed or not, he had a dad already. Joss shook his head at Sirus, his words bitter. "Well you're not like a father to me. I already have a father. Remember?"

"Yes, but I thought . . ." The light in Sirus's eyes changed then, as if something had just been answered for him. He seemed sad, but at the same time, strangely at peace. Joss wondered what he was thinking. "It doesn't matter what I thought. I never did anything purposefully to hurt you, Joss. I need you to trust me on that."

"Why? Why should I trust a monster like you?"

"Because you're the only one who knows that I'm alive who still has the ability to see past the fangs to the man beneath this vampire exterior." Sirus shook his head and stepped closer, placing a caring hand on Joss's shoulder. As he squeezed it, he said, "I'm not just a vampire, Joss, and I think you know that. I'm Sirus. And I never stopped caring about you."

It might have been a mistake to believe Sirus. But Joss couldn't help it. He believed every word, and at the moment, he didn't give a crap if he only believed because of vampire mind control or some other super-natural thought manipulation. He believed Sirus. And

Joss was relieved to have Sirus back in his life. He could only imagine how Sirus's daughter would feel in the same situation. "Does Kat know that you're still alive?"

"No." Sirus released a breath and seemed to relax some.

"Why haven't you told her yet?"

"I'm worried about her reaction. Kat wants me to go through with our plans to turn her into a vampire, and I cannot bear the thought of that sweet girl becoming what I have become. I just can't take the idea of her doing all that I have done, simply in the name of survival. Not to mention the politics."

"If that's the issue—and trust me, I'm not saying it's a good idea to turn your daughter into a blood-sucking creature of the night—then why not just find some other vampire to turn her?" It seemed simple enough. But then, if it were really that simple, why hadn't Kat just found a vampire to turn her already? Especially since she was under the impression that her dad was dead?

"I know Kat." Sirus sighed. "She'd only ever turn if it was by her father's doing."

"She'd understand, you know. If you took the time to explain it to her. She'd probably be so relieved that you're still alive that she'd forget all about becoming a vampire herself." That's what Joss was hoping, anyway. Kat could be pretty scary as a human. As a vampire? She'd be unstoppable.

"You think so?" Joss nodded in response, and Sirus took a moment to consider this. Then he shook his head, his shoulders weighed down by guilt. "Losing me has probably affected her in the worst ways . . ."

"Well, she's kinda been stalking me. I think she intends to kill me. Or take my cousin away. Or something. I'm not sure." He shrugged, hoping that Sirus would help him somehow. If anyone could talk some sense into Kat, it was Sirus.

Sirus nodded and patted Joss on the back. "Maybe I can talk some sense into her. Will you come with me, so I can reveal myself to her and explain everything?"

"Of course, Sirus." A smile found its way to Joss's lips at last. Maybe everything really was going to be okay, after all. As they moved toward the edge of the forest, Joss cast Sirus a sidelong glance and said, "Hey, what did you mean when you said to trust my dreams?"

But Sirus didn't have a chance to answer. Something unseen whipped between them, brushing Joss's hair back from his forehead for a second, and the next thing Joss knew, Sirus was lying on the forest floor, coughing. Blood lined his lips. Fear filled his eyes. And the last thing that Joss noticed before the light left his mentor's eyes was Joss's own stake sticking out of Sirus's chest. His body fell still, and Joss felt a black cloud of sorrow envelope his soul.

Sirus was gone. For real this time. And it had been at Joss's hand, in a way. If Joss hadn't brought a weapon of vampire destruction into this scenario, maybe Sirus would still be alive. If Joss hadn't . . .

It was his fault. It was all his fault.

Joss moved to Sirus and dropped to his knees. There was a brief moment, as he stretched his hand forward to check for a pulse, when Joss thought that maybe it had all been a dream—a horrific nightmare and soon he'd awaken in his bed. But the second his fingers touched the part of Sirus's neck where his carotid artery should have been pulsing, all of Joss's hopes flew away, like a puff of smoke. Sirus was dead.

His chest seized. His vision blurred. He whipped his head around, trying to get a look at Sirus's killer, but he was alone in the woods, alone in life, alone in his grief. And he had lost his father figure for the second time.

· 14 ·

THE ONSET OF UNDERSTANDING

The morning sun poured in through Joss's window the following day, but he didn't get out of bed, and only barely moved, just enough to lift his head and gaze at his window, guessing that it was at least nine, and maybe something closer to ten o'clock. He'd spent much of the night searching the woods for Sirus's killer, and when the sun had hinted that it might soon come up, he'd begrudgingly made his way home. The moment his head had hit the pillow, he was out. Insomnia usually occupied his nights, but strangely, in his grief, Joss had found the ability to sleep deeply. Maybe it was his subconscious's way of protecting him from the pain that he felt while he was awake. Or maybe it was his body's way of just shutting down until Joss figured out exactly how to deal with how much he was hurting over the death of Sirus.

It really made him think about his mom and dad, and how they were dealing with the death of Cecile by not dealing with it at all.

He watched those curtains for a while, blocking out all thought, and finally, Joss sat up in bed. It was time to begin his day, grief or no grief. After a quick, hot shower, he dressed and made his way silently down the stairs.

His mom was sitting at the dining room table, a steaming mug of coffee clutched in her hand. There was no sign of his dad or Henry, for which he was extremely grateful. He sat down in the chair across from his mother and folded his fingers together, silently musing precisely how he should begin.

As if waking from a deep daydream, his mother blinked and finally took notice of him. "Oh. Good morning, Joss. Sleep okay?"

It was a brief moment of clarity in her medication-induced fog. Joss knew that he'd better seize the moment, before she was lost to him again. "Not really. I don't usually sleep very well."

"Nightmares?" The question rolled off her tongue as if she were well aware of his nocturnal issues. But she wasn't. Of that he was almost certain.

"No. Not last night."

"That's good." She put the mug to her lips and sipped. When she spoke again, her voice was hushed in concern. "Sometimes I hear you cry out at night. I worry . . ."

A lump appeared in Joss's throat. She worried about him. He honestly hadn't thought that she was capable of that anymore. He'd thought that she was lost to him forever, the way that Cecile was. The way that Sirus was.

He stretched his right hand out slowly and took his mom's hand in his. It took a second, but she finally met his eyes. They sat there in silence, holding hands. Joss spent those moments searching for the right words. Finally, when he thought that maybe he'd found them, he began. "I dream about Cecile sometimes. About what happened. I blame myself for her dying. And I blame her death for our family being so broken. Sometimes I wonder if a person can ever really heal after losing someone to death. Sometimes I wonder if I'll ever get over that feeling of loss. Do you . . . ever think about things like that?"

Her eyes shimmered as she squeezed Joss's hand. She pulled her hand away and picked up her coffee mug once again, sipping its contents quietly.

Joss wanted an answer. More than that, he needed

an answer. He needed to know that he wasn't the only one who felt so alone, so broken after death had infected his life. He needed to be understood.

As he opened his mouth again, to tell her precisely that, he noticed that the haze had returned to her eyes. His mother was gone again, her mind hiding in whatever place it hid when pain breached her perimeter. The sight of that haze in her eyes angered him. But more than that, it hurt him. Especially when he looked at the prescription bottles on the table. "Mom . . . I wish you wouldn't take so many pills."

"I have to. The doctor says the medication helps me, Joss." Her voice was even, almost robotic.

Fury welled up inside of Joss then, and before he knew what he was doing, he picked up the bottles from the table and whipped them across the room, smashing them against the wall. The lids popped surprisingly easily from the plastic containers and pills flew everywhere. Joss shouted, "They don't help anything!"

His mom's robotic stare turned to him for the moment, and Joss knew that he had to get out of that room before he tried to shake the sanity back into her.

"It doesn't help you, Mom. The stupid medication doesn't help you at all. It makes you different." He stood, but just as he'd begun to turn away, he turned back to face his mother. He leaned down, meeting her eyes so that he could be sure that she heard him. "I miss the way you used to be. Before Cecile died."

As he stepped outside, he inhaled the fresh air and focused on how it made him physically feel. He could focus on the physical. Just not the emotional. Not now. Even though that was all his suffering mind seemed to want to notice.

His walk to Paty's cottage was brief, but blissfully uneventful. He was relieved not to encounter anyone along the way. Joss didn't feel much like talking. Even inane chitchat didn't appeal to him as he moved from his house to his fellow Slayer's temporary quarters. All he wanted was silence, and the ability to forget.

Silence was all he was given by whatever force makes the Universe operate. It was enough, for the moment.

Before he could knock on Paty's door, she opened it, as if she'd been awaiting his arrival. She met Joss's surprised expression with a smile. "I'm so glad you're here, Joss. I'm bored out of my skull. Come on in. You hungry? I was just getting ready to make a sandwich. Want one?"

She led him inside and started gathering items from the refrigerator without waiting for his response. Joss followed her, taking his seat at the counter. As she moved about the kitchen, creating a lunchtime masterpiece, Paty hummed, happy to have something to do and someone to take care of. Joss didn't have the heart to tell her that the last thing he wanted to do was eat anything. Sorrow had a funny way of erasing even the healthiest teenage boy's appetite. But Paty treated him like a son, and when a mother's son needed to eat but didn't feel like it, she fed him.

The plate that Paty set in front of him moments later was small and white, with a thin silver line along its rim. Sitting on it was the thickest turkey sandwich that Joss had ever seen. A pile of thinly sliced turkey breast, fresh lettuce, sliced green peppers, and yellow mustard all between two slices of Italian bread. Beside the sandwich was a pickle, and beside that was a handful of potato chips. Joss bet that it would be delicious. He just wasn't hungry enough to find out. Still, he nodded his gratitude to Paty, who was chomping into her sandwich, identical to his, while standing across the counter from him. "Thanks, Paty. Looks good."

She nodded and chewed, and after a moment, cocked an eyebrow. She set her sandwich on a plate just like Joss's and leaned over the counter, eyeballing him. "Something's wrong. What's happened, Joss? You look like you just lost your best friend."

The lump in Joss's throat grew, choking him, but he managed to subdue it. But when he spoke, his voice cracked, hinting at the sadness that was going to break him into pieces at any moment. "I met with Sirus yesterday."

"Oh? How'd it go?"

"He's dead."

She paused, but only briefly. "Congratulations."

"Not by me. Someone—something—else killed him. They used my stake."

"I'll report his demise to the Society this afternoon." She seemed so casual, so flippant, as if they were discussing the death of a housefly. The crack in Joss's heart widened into a chasm. He didn't know why he'd expected Paty to be sympathetic, to hug him and tell him that it was okay to miss Sirus and that everything would be okay somehow. She was a Slayer. Of course she didn't care about the death of yet another vampire. "So did you find what killed him and take care of it? Because whatever killed him likely killed those other people."

"I'm aware of that. And no. I looked for it, but couldn't find anything." He bent forward, resting his cheek on counter and fighting off the tears that threatened to pour down his cheeks. In his mind, all he could see was his stake sticking out of Sirus's chest, out of Vlad's back. Maybe Henry was right. Maybe he was the monster, after all. Maybe all Slayers were really just monsters.

Paty lifted the lid off the cookie jar and retrieved a

chocolate chip cookie. As she set it in front of the still-not-hungry Joss, she asked, "How's the rest of your summer going?"

After a long moment, Joss sat up again, breaking the cookie in half. He didn't eat any of it, but instead took his time reducing it to tiny bits of cookie on his plate. The act of destruction was strangely comforting to him. He wondered what that said about him as a person. "My summer. Let's see. My cousin Henry's been a pain. I mean, I really like him, but he's pretty convinced that I'm evil to the core for being a Slayer."

Echoing his words in his mind was the afterthought, *"And I'm worried he might be right."*

Paty took the sliced pickle from Joss's plate and bit into it, nodding. "People get some messed up convictions once they're exposed to the existence of vampires."

Joss watched her for a little while, and finally, in a burst of quiet courage, he whispered, "I think the Society is right to be concerned about me and my loyalty to the cause, Paty."

She looked at him then, and it was as if she'd finally really, truly looked at him for the first time. He saw empathy in her eyes, and the mothering concern that he'd been hoping to find. She reached across the counter and gave his arm a light squeeze. "Don't worry about that right now, Joss. You're still in shock over the whole Sirus thing. But you've got a job to do—

an important job. Just let it go and focus on finding out whomever or whatever is killing people in Santa Carla. You've got more information now, more clues. You're a Slayer. Do your job and stop mourning a dead vampire."

Her words struck him painfully, solidly in the chest. Let it never be said that Paty was shy or demure about her opinions.

She was right, of course. And Joss had never been one to lose himself in grief, but instead to fight his way out of it, so the advice that she'd given him was solid. That didn't mean that his heart wasn't cracked or that he was going to leap from his chair and break into song, but it did help in some strange way. He nodded the gratitude to Paty that he could not form on his tongue and popped the last uncrushed bit of cookie into his mouth. He wasn't hungry yet, but he was getting there.

From the other end of the house, the dryer buzzer went off. Paty sighed and looked at him. "I'll be right back, okay? Don't go anywhere just yet."

He nodded that he wouldn't leave, and after she stepped out of the room, Joss noticed her cell phone sitting on the counter. He knew that he shouldn't do what he was thinking of doing, but feeling like a monster was weighing on him. Chastising himself for what he was about to do, he picked up the phone and scrolled through Paty's contacts until he came to Morgan's number. With a deep breath, he pressed the Call button and put the phone to his ear.

Two rings. Three. Maybe Morgan wasn't home. Maybe Morgan was too busy being a good Slayer to answer.

A gruff voice cut on the line. "Paty? What's up?"

At first, Joss didn't answer. Of course Morgan would think that it would be Paty calling. It was her phone, after all. He thought about hanging up then—maybe Paty and Morgan would blame the call on a butt dial or something—but then Morgan said, "Is Joss okay?"

No. Joss wasn't okay. He needed to talk to a friend, because he was having some serious doubts about what it was to be a Slayer, in service to the Society. On the other end, Morgan was growing impatient. "Hello?"

Joss gripped the cell phone in his hand, not knowing when Paty might walk back into the room. "Hey, Morgan. It's . . . it's me. Joss."

"Joss?" Morgan grew quiet then, and Joss wasn't sure if he'd done the right thing by calling him. Then Morgan said, "Paty okay?"

"Yeah. I just needed to talk. And my phone is . . . unavailable." His chest felt tight. It felt like he was lying, but he wasn't. And he didn't plan to. He just had to be very careful what he said over the phone. In case the Society was listening.

Morgan paused. "I see. Well . . . what can I help you with?"

Joss pinched the bridge of his nose with his free hand. After a moment, he whispered, "Do you ever wonder if we're on the right side?"

Morgan grew quiet. Joss was putting him on the spot, and in a potentially difficult situation. Joss didn't blame him for not answering right away. He wouldn't blame Morgan if he didn't answer at all, if he simply hung up the phone and reported Joss's doubts to the Society elders. But then Morgan said, "Wondering that would be considered blasphemy in the eyes of the Slayer Society, little brother."

Reading between the lines, Joss saw that Morgan was saying that yes, he'd wondered that, too, at times. He was telling Joss that he understood without actually saying it. Smart guy. "It certainly would."

"Wanna know what I think?" There was a rustling as Morgan adjusted his phone, followed by determined words. "I think there are no good sides to be on. I think a real man makes his own choices. I think you know what path is right for you, and you don't have to follow one that's been handed to you. You got it?"

Joss took in a deep breath and blew it out slowly, feeling a little less alone in his confusion. "Got it."

Morgan sighed. "We could both be in a lot of trouble for this little chat, Joss."

"I know. I'm sorry." There was so much that Joss wanted to say to Morgan, so much that he wanted to ask. But someone could be listening. Almost in an afterthought, he asked, "How's your brother?"

Joss could almost hear Morgan smile on the other end. "He's good, Joss. How's your friend?"

Friend. He was asking about Vlad. Joss furrowed his brow. Was Vlad his friend? Was Morgan insinuating that he was? "I . . . don't know."

"Maybe, next time you see him, you should find out."

Joss parted his lips to say that he would, but Paty walked in then with a full basket of laundry and dropped it on the floor beside the couch. Joss hit the End button and set her phone discretely back on the counter where he'd taken it from. His conversation with Morgan, for the moment, was finished.

"Listen, Joss." She returned to her spot in the kitchen and lowered her voice until Joss had to strain to hear it. "From here on out, I want you to debrief me every night, until the killer's been found and dealt with. And I think it's a good idea if you stick fairly close to your cousin. You just never know what danger he might find himself in, you know?"

"Sure." Joss furrowed his brow. Paty had never seemed so concerned about Henry before. How strange. "If you think that's best."

"I do." She darted her eyes around the room briefly, as if concerned that someone might hear their exchange. At this, Joss stood and made his way to the door.

"Thanks for the sandwich. I'd better get back. My mom's probably wondering where I went." It wasn't true, of course. But there was something strange about the way that Paty was acting that made Joss want to put some distance between the two of them. Why was she acting like Henry could be in danger? Did she know something that Joss didn't?

He thought about their exchange on the walk home, but it wasn't long before his thoughts switched gears. As he walked in the door, Henry rushed by him and out the door. Joss looked at his mom, who was sitting at the kitchen table, staring into a hot cup of tea, and said, "What's his hurry?"

"Hmm?" She glanced up at him, as if she hadn't been fully aware of his presence at all until just that moment. "Oh . . . Henry's got a date this afternoon. He's taking some girl to see a movie, I think."

Concern burned on Joss's edges like flame on paper. "What girl?"

She dipped her tea bag into the cup and then wrung it out and set it on the saucer. "I think he said her name is Kat. Or Kathy. Or Katherine. Something like that."

Without another word to his mom, Joss headed

out the door, letting the screen bang closed. Grounded or not, he was leaving this house.

He caught up to Henry just passed the mailbox. Henry looked freshly showered and ready for an afternoon with the fairer sex. "What are you doing?"

Henry smirked as they walked toward town. "Wishing I had transportation other than my feet."

"You're going to a movie?"

Henry shrugged. "Yeah. *Mangled Zombie Pirates from Outer Space* comes out today. Catching a matinee."

"With who?"

"Not that it's any of your business, but I'm meeting Kat there."

Joss stepped in front of his cousin and stopped him with a hand to the chest. He had to say something, had to protect Henry from the potential danger that he was putting himself in by entering a dark room with Kat. What if she meant to kill Henry, just to get back at Joss for Sirus's demise? The theater would be a good place to do it. "Henry, you can't go out with Kat. You don't understand. She's just using you to get to me."

"Well, look who just gnawed his way through the straps." Henry shook his head and moved around his cousin. "Seriously, Joss. That's not even remotely possible."

"She thought I killed her dad a few summers ago and she's been out for revenge ever since."

"And she hopes to accomplish this by making out

with your cousin in a dark theater?" Henry slowed his steps for a moment, as if considering this possibility. Then, as if reaching a conclusion, he smiled and continued walking. "I'm game."

"Don't do this, Henry. Please. I'm asking you not to." He tugged his cousin's sleeve until Henry stopped to face him. Joss was relieved to see honest consideration there. Henry seemed torn between a pretty face and family loyalty. Joss shook his head, keeping his voice soft. "You should just choose your friends more wisely, y'know?"

A glimmer of anger crossed Henry's eyes then and Joss instantly regretted his own words. Henry shook him off and crossed the street to the awaiting theater. As he did so, he shouted over his shoulder, "You almost had me, Joss. But no."

Waiting for him at the ticket window was Kat. She was dressed in cutoff jean shorts, Converse sneakers that had seen better days, and a T-shirt that read "What I really need are Minions." As she and Henry disappeared into the theater, she smiled and gave Joss a little wave.

Joss didn't pause, not even for a microsecond. Instead, he crossed the street to the ticket booth, dug a crumpled ten-dollar bill from out of his jeans pocket, and slapped it on the counter. "One for the *Mangled Teenage Zombie Pilots* flick, or whatever it's called."

The boy inside the ticket booth rolled his eyes. "You mean *Mangled Zombie Pirates from Outer Space.* Come on, dude. If you're not gonna take the genre seriously, at least get the title right."

Fighting the urge to throw a sarcastic quip the guy's way, Joss quietly accepted his ticket and moved to the door of the theater. A bored-looking girl in a uniform that was two sizes too big for her took his ticket and ripped off the stub at the end before letting him inside. She pointed behind herself to the left and sighed her directions, "Theater five. That way."

Passing through the people who were buying snacks at the snack counter or just hanging out, waiting for friends or whatever Hollywood masterpiece was coming up next in theaters one through eight, Joss made his way to theater five and moved inside. It was very dark and the previews were already playing, but it didn't take long for him to locate Henry and Kat. Mostly because they were attached at the face.

He took a seat three rows behind them, telling himself that it would be a smart idea to just watch how things played out, rather than jump in the middle of their date and prove Henry's Joss-is-a-jerk theory right. After the preview for a sappy romantic comedy about a divorced couple inheriting a bunny farm, they played a gorgeous trailer about a boy who falls for a witch or something in this messed up southern town and another trailer about this girl who fought giant blue monsters off with only a katana. Joss was a million percent positive that he was going to pass on the bunnies, but witches and katanas sounded just like what the doctor ordered.

After the previews, the movie finally began, but Joss couldn't stop himself from keeping a close eye on Henry and Kat. On one hand, it was weird to see them kissing, to see his two worlds colliding—once again through his cousin. On the other, it sent a wave of sadness through him. He wished so badly that he could, just for a few hours, forget about vampires and the Society's rules, and all that came with being a Slayer and just snuggle with a pretty girl in a dark movie theater, not knowing or caring what might be waiting for them outside in the light of day. He wished so terribly that he could just be a normal teenager, and not be forced to keep those he cared about at arms' length. It would be nice not to constantly be on the verge of an argument with Henry. It would be nice to be cuddled up with Meredith in the movie theater, her head on his shoulder, the real world a million miles from their collective thoughts. It would be so nice that it pained Joss to even think of it for a brief moment. Because it could never happen. There would never be peace. There would never be a moment like that between him and Meredith. Never.

He slumped in his seat and forced his eyes to the screen, so jealous and bitter and just plain sad that all he wanted was to forget about Henry and Kat for five minutes and just lose himself in the make-believe of Hollywood. So he did for a while. But his Slayer mind kept dragging his attention back to the seemingly happy couple, just in case something started to go horrifically wrong and Joss had a chance to rescue Henry from Kat's sordid plans. After some time though, during one of those stints where Joss found himself lost in the film and the impressive special effects, he glanced down at their seats and found them missing. Panic spread through his chest and he jumped up from his seat, hurrying out of theater five and out of the movie theater altogether.

The sun blinded him as he burst through the doors, but his eyes adjusted quickly. He searched the area, but found no trace, no sign of either Kat or his cousin. Moving back to the ticket booth, he looked at the boy inside. "Hey, have you seen a couple walk out of here? She was wearing some shirt that said something about Minions . . . ?"

The guy blinked. At first Joss wasn't certain that he'd been listening, but then—as if he spent most of his days walking around in a kind of half coma—the guy said, "Oh them? Yeah. I think they went behind the theater."

"Thanks." Hurrying around the building, the two sides of Joss's brain began having an argument. One side, the Slayer side, was convinced that Joss would find Henry dead at the vengeful hands of Kat. The other side said that that was a paranoid thought process and the most he was likely to find were two teenagers making out in the alley behind the theater. Joss just wished that they'd both shut up and let him do the thinking on his own from here on out.

He also realized that that made no sense at all.

As Joss rounded the building, he saw Henry facing Kat with his hands held up in front of him. Kat was brandishing a switchblade knife, its blade glinting in the midday sun. Henry gasped as he spoke. "Is this because I bit your tongue?"

"Are you dense?" She shook her head, but held her grip on the weapon in her hand. "I don't want to do this, Henry. You're a really sweet guy. But you're also someone Joss cares about and losing you will tear him apart. And that's exactly what your cousin deserves. Pain. Like no other. Like the pain that he inflicted on me. Killing him isn't enough. I wouldn't feel better after simply taking his life. I have to hurt him. Because he hurt me in the worst way imaginable. You have no idea what he's done to me, the pain I've felt."

"Joss told me not to trust you. He said he killed your dad or something." The last sentence came out sounding more like a question. Joss lurked at the corner of the building, strategizing. But eavesdropping, too.

Kat's eyes immediately welled with tears. It would have been amazing to reunite her with her father. But whatever lurked in the woods had taken his life, and now Kat would never believe Joss that he hadn't actually killed Sirus.

As Kat wiped at her eyes with her free hand, she said, "He did. Sirus was a vampire and Joss killed him. Because it's what they do. Slayers. They can't see past their rules and murderous solutions. They're evil. All of them."

"Not Joss." Henry dropped his hands and shook his head, his tone confident. It surprised the hell out of Joss to hear his words. But it surprised him more to hear Henry's conviction. "My cousin may be a lot of things. He may make some really messed up choices now and again. But he's one of the good guys. He just can't see it yet. Because that stupid Slayer Society has him so confused."

Kat snorted. "Believe what you want, Henry. Slayers aren't any good at all. Vampires, on the other hand—"

"Not all vampires are good, Kat. I mean, my best friend is a vampire and he's awesome. But there are plenty of evil vampires in the world. Just like there are both good and bad Slayers in the world. Just like there are good and bad people in the world. There's no difference." Henry was trying to reach her, to make her see the world the way that he did. In that moment, Joss realized that his cousin, for all of his stupid faults, was one of the smartest people that Joss had ever known.

She set her jaw then and, after a moment, moved closer. With every step she took, Joss's heart picked up its pace. Stealthily, he stepped away from the building, matching her pace. She had her eyes locked on Henry the entire time. Without warning, she bolted forward and grabbed Henry by the wrist with her free hand. In one fluid motion, she flipped him over her shoulder. Henry went down, landing on his back in the dirt, sending up a smattering of dust.

Kat had clearly been training. Hard.

A worried tickle crawled up Joss's spine. It grew the moment that Kat climbed on top of Henry and moved the knife from her left hand to her right hand. Kat was stronger than he'd imagined. Not as strong as a vampire, but maybe as strong as a Slayer. Plus, she was fast. Maybe too fast. It was going to be a challenge for him to subdue her. Surprise would have to be on his side.

"I have to do this. I'm sorry." She said to Henry that she was sorry, but her movements suggested that she was anything but. She pulled her arm back to thrust the blade into Henry's chest. The metal gleamed in the sunlight, a sharp threat in the broad light of day. Henry stirred, but he was clearly dazed.

As fast as he could move, Joss ran toward Kat. He had to remove her from the equation, protect his cousin, but do so without causing her any permanent damage. Kat wasn't evil—despite what her immediate actions might suggest—but she was confused. And she was dangerous.

Hoping she had not yet noticed him trailing her, Joss grabbed her wrist and snapped it back, breaking it smoothly. Kat let out a small cry of surprise and pain, immediately holding her wrist to her chest and cradling it in her free hand. The knife fell to the ground, and Joss kicked it away.

For a moment, Joss thought that he'd neutralized the situation completely. But then Kat jumped up, turned on him, and kicked her foot high, aiming for his chest. At the last second, he dodged her advance and spun away from her. Kat, it seemed, wouldn't be so easily deterred.

As he spun around and reached for her, Henry appeared behind her. He picked Kat up in a wrestling move that would have made John Cena proud, flipping her over his shoulder. Kat hit the brick wall of the building and fell into an unconscious heap.

Joss stood there marveling at how he'd thought his

cousin had needed protection, and so relieved that he hadn't had to hurt Kat any more than he had. Henry was standing there, looking more than a little upset. Joss patted Henry on the shoulder. "You okay?"

Henry released a sigh, shaking his head at Kat's unconscious form. "She was going to kill me, Joss. You saw. I had no choice."

"Hey." He made sure that Henry was looking at him before he spoke again. His cousin's fingers were trembling. Joss's weren't. "You had no choice. She *was* going to kill you, Henry. But we stopped her. You stopped her."

Henry's eyes found Kat once again. He nodded slowly. "Yeah. You're right. Are you . . . are you okay?"

Joss nodded. He was okay. He was better than okay. He was finally beginning to understand his cousin.

A breeze blew through the alley and, as it did, Henry seemed to lose his footing. He fell over in a pile beside Kat, and before Joss could inquire, something had Joss by the throat. It lifted him high into the air, flying over buildings and trees, until finally, it dropped him into the woods. The invisible force tossed him against a tree trunk, and then another, until Joss's lungs seized and his every muscle hurt. At last, it threw him against a large oak and his skull cracked against the wood. Darkness overtook Joss. And all that was waiting for him in that darkness was confusion.

▶ **15** ◀

DREAM TIME

Light swirled slowly around Joss once again and, as he looked up at his attacker, a strange calm overtook him. A calm that came solely from understanding that he was once more locked inside a dream.

Cecile stood over him, dressed in a pretty white dress, a blue silk ribbon tied around her waist, with matching ribbons in her hair, tangled in her blond curls. Her feet were bare, her hands clean, and her eyes . . .

Joss furrowed his brow a bit at the strangeness of what he saw. Cecile's eyes were not black at all. They were not soulless tunnels that sent a terrified chill through his core. Her eyes were blue. Crystalline blue, as they'd been when she was still alive. And beautiful.

As he gazed up at her, he noticed that her eyes were narrowed at him, almost fierce, as if she weren't entirely happy to see him. He parted his lips to say something—anything would have done, simply to break the unnerving silence—but when he did, she opened her mouth, revealing two fangs hidden within. She snapped her teeth at him in a threatening bite and Joss closed his mouth again, settling back against the tree behind him. This was the strangest dream he'd ever had about his little sister, and he was seriously looking forward to waking up.

They remained that way for several minutes, each examining the other in silence, until finally Joss could bear the quiet no more. In dreams past, asking Cecile a question had launched his subconscious into all sorts of horrific images, but Joss knew that this was simply a part of his dreams, and the way that they were meant to play out. So with a slow, deep breath, he prepared himself for the nightmarish inevitable, and said, "What are you doing here, Cecile?"

Tilting her head to the side, as if she were a little taken aback to hear her name leave his lips, Cecile spoke—her voice sweet and lyrical, despite the fact that her words were ominous and dark. "I have a job to do. A very important job that Em gave me."

Upon hearing Em's name—a creature well documented to be the oldest living vampire in existence—the tiny hairs on the back of Joss's neck stood on end. Normally his dreams didn't contain such details from his waking life. Normally they were filled to the brim with blood and fear and his guilt over having failed to save his sister. This nightmare was a strange one, for sure. He met her eyes and held her gaze. "Oh? What job did Em give you to do?"

Sunshine was filtering through the treetops, warming Joss's shoulders some. A light breeze rustled the woods slightly, the scent of something floral and wild carried on its surface. It was a pleasant day . . . for not being a day at all. Not really. Joss couldn't wrap his head around the direction of his nightmare, but he was trusting that he'd see where it was headed soon. Cecile's hands would become filthy claws. Her eyes would swirl into evil, black tunnels. And Joss's heart would break into a million guilty pieces. It happened. Every time he dreamed about Cecile, it happened.

"I killed Sirus."

At her words, Joss's jaw fell open. Such a cruel reminder of his subconscious that Sirus was dead. Joss shook his head, his response a whisper. "Did you, now?"

"He'd betrayed her one too many times. She said she couldn't trust him anymore, that no one in Elysia could. He had to be stopped." She nodded, her blond curls bouncing on her shoulders, her pretty eyes so large. Light freckles dotted her nose. Everything but the fangs in her mouth and the words escaping her lips suggested that she was still the same, sweet girl that he had known and loved. She whispered, as if someone might overhear and she wanted this moment to be private between the two of them. "Now Em wants me to kill you, too."

The ache in the back of his head from hitting the tree trunk throbbed, and Joss reached up to rub it thoughtfully. Everything about this dream told him that he wasn't dreaming at all. Was that even a possibility? Cecile was dead.

Wasn't she?

If Cecile was somehow crazily still alive, if she'd actually survived that night of terror from so long ago, it all made perfect sense. A vampire had been killing people in Santa Carla, but the murders had been performed in a way that suggested inexperience. Messy— much like the crayon drawings that Cecile used to make for him. She'd been feeding here in Santa Carla and waiting to do a job for Em, waiting for Sirus and her brother. Waiting to kill.

He looked into her eyes, examined her lovely face, marveled at the features that were so like his own, a perfect blending of their parents. Cecile was alive. She was a vampire, but she was alive. He hadn't allowed her to die after all. "Cecile . . . do you . . . do you remember me?"

She knelt in front of him then and stretched her hand forward, caressing his cheek in such a sweet gesture that Joss felt his eyes moisten with tears. "Of course. Of course I remember you, Jossie. I could never forget my big brother."

His tears spilled forth at last and he placed a hand over Cecile's, closing his eyes. She was all right. He hadn't let her die. She was alive, after all.

"But that doesn't change anything. I have a job to do, Jossie. A very important job." She pulled her hand away and stood, regret and confusion filling her features. Behind it was determination. "I have to do it. I just have to."

Joss blinked up at her, only vaguely aware of the building fire in her gaze. A fire he had seen before, from creatures of her kind. "What job, Cecile? What are you talking about?"

"It's too late for talking, Jossie. It's too late for everything now." Her words, at first, were hushed. But they soon gave way to a tone that sent a shiver down Joss's spine. "It's time for you to die, big brother."

Terror enveloped him then. But not at the stance that she'd taken, the words that she'd spoken, or the fangs inside her mouth. Terror enveloped him the moment that he became acutely aware of the wooden stake in the holster on his hip, and he realized that he was going to have to use it.

▸ 16 ◂

REASONING WITH CECILE

ecile parted her lips, revealing the sharp fangs hidden inside of her mouth. Joss closed his eyes for the briefest of moments, trying to regain his composure and to find his inner strength for what he needed to do. As he took a deep breath, the sweet smell of vanilla filled his nose. Cecile had always loved the smell of vanilla. She used to take the bottle when their mom was baking cookies and dab a drop behind her ear, like she had seen her mother do with perfume.

When Joss opened his eyes again, the scene hadn't changed. Cecile was still standing over him. Her dress blew in the breeze and her fangs glinted in the sunlight. Joss moved to sit up but a surging pain in the back of his head prevented that from happening. His hand quickly found its way to the source of the pain, a large swollen lump under his hair. A lump from where his head had hit the tree.

A sudden realization fell over him. Joss sat up, in spite of the pain. "Cecile, what's wrong with your eyes?"

Cecile furrowed her brow and pursed her lips. "What do you mean? There's nothing wrong with my eyes."

She was absolutely right. Her eyes were almost perfect. Deep, bright, and blue. Not the soulless, black chasms that Joss had come to know in his dreams. The only difference in these eyes from when Joss had last seen them in person was that the innocence held within them was gone. Joss finally knew why they hadn't changed. Because he wasn't dreaming. One nightmare had finally come to an end. Another, it seemed, was just beginning.

"I'm sorry, Cecile!" Joss held his hands up in front of him, pleading. Cecile was a vampire, so he had no doubts whatsoever that she would follow through with her attack, that she would take the life of her brother, a Slayer. But this was his last chance to say the words that had been circling his mind ever since the night. "I'm sorry that I didn't investigate further that night and learn that you hadn't been killed, but turned into a vampire. I'm sorry I didn't have strong enough instincts to determine that something was off about you that night, and to do everything that I could to track down the vampire who'd bit you. I'm sorry. Believe me. I'm so sorry."

Cecile's fangs shrank slowly back into her gums. She tilted her head, her eyes shimmering and focused on her brother. "Why, Jossie? Why didn't you save me that night?"

Joss shook his head. "I couldn't, Cecile. I couldn't. By the time I saw you—"

"I wasn't a vampire yet." She stomped her foot in a way that reminded Joss of the few temper tantrums that Cecile had ever thrown. She was angry, but she was angry like his sister had been and less like the vampire that she had become.

"I thought you were dead." His words were a whisper. As he spoke them, images from the night he'd lost her flashed through his mind. Joss creeping down the hall. Cecile lying on her bed, pale, still. The thin line of blood tracing down her cheek to her pink ballerina sheets. The monster looming over her. It felt like yesterday. "Besides, I was just a boy. A frightened boy who could only sit in the corner and cry and be scared. I couldn't save you then. . . ."

Tears welled up in Joss's eyes, blurring his vision. But not so much that he couldn't see Cecile move toward him. She threw herself into his arms, clinging to him, soaking the shoulder of his shirt with her tears. Joss embraced her, hugging her so tightly to him that it almost erased from his mind what he was about to do. Almost. ". . . but I can save you now."

In an action that threatened to shrivel his very soul, Joss reached down to the holster on his hip and gripped his stake tightly. As he pulled it upward, freeing it from its leather constraints, he told himself that he was doing the right thing. He told himself that the creature that was clutching him so closely wasn't really his sister at all, but a monster. He told himself that Cecile was better off not living than living as a vampire. He didn't truly believe any of those things, but he told himself those things over and over again, hoping that somehow, someday, he would come to believe them.

He lifted the stake, uselessly fighting his tears as he gauged the best entry point to reach her heart. Gripping his weapon tightly, Joss squeezed his eyes shut and whispered into her sweet smelling hair, "For you, Cecile."

· 17 ·

AN UNEXPECTED RELATIONSHIP

Joss brought his stake down hard and fast, promising himself that he wouldn't miss, swearing to himself that he was doing the right thing by ending the vampire Cecile's young life. As his weapon whipped through the air, tears spilled down his cheeks in anguish. Cecile was alive, in a way. She'd been alive this entire time. And he was about to cause her death— the thing that had been the catalyst in his becoming a vampire Slayer in the first place. Irony weighed heavily on him. Almost as heavily as the guilt that was overflowing from within him.

The stake flew toward Cecile's back, but just before

it made contact, something hit Joss hard in the wrist. He lost his grip and the stake went flying several yards to his right, landing in a tall patch of grass. Joss darted his eyes to the left, to locate whoever or whatever had disarmed him, the night air coolly brushing his bangs to the side. It took a moment to recognize the facial features. It took less time for a cloud of confusion to form inside his mind. Blinking, his eyes found the stake again before returning to Paty, who was standing beside him, chest heaving, eyes full of tears. "Paty, what are you—"

"Leave her alone, Joss." Paty crouched and took Cecile into her arms, almost snatching her away from her brother. As she stood, she smoothed Cecile's blond curls back from her surprised face.

Joss slowly got to his feet, a strange new tension flooding through his body as he looked at his fellow Slayer cradling his younger sister in her arms. "What are you doing?"

Paty set Cecile on the ground and moved in front of her, her moist eyes furious as she turned them on Joss. "I swear, if you as much as touch Cecile once more, I'll rip your heart out!"

Joss glanced down at Cecile, who was now standing behind Paty, looking angrily at him, as if he'd done the unforgivable. He'd never been more confused. "Paty, you don't know what's going on here."

"The hell I don't." Her tone was bitter and sharp. Every word slashed through Joss's resolve to stay calm.

He released a deep breath, urging his muscles to relax. This was Paty. He trusted her. So why did he feel so on edge? "How do you know my sister?"

"I know Cecile better than anyone. I'm sworn to protect her . . ." Paty straightened her shoulders with a sense of dignity, devotion, and pride. ". . . as her drudge."

Drudge. Joss knew that word very well. It was a word that had been used to describe his cousin Henry. It was a word that meant that Paty was a vampire's human slave. His sister's human slave.

Absolute fury enveloped him then, like hot flames licking up his form. "How did this happen?"

"Late last summer, the day we were all packing up to leave New York, the day before we flew out, I'd decided to duck out and pick up a gift for my niece at the last minute. My shopping trip ended up taking a while and by the time I was heading back to head-quarters, the sun was going down. On my way back, I saw a girl. She was just sitting on the sidewalk, cry-ing." Paty looked down at Cecile then, who curled her tiny fingers around Paty's hand, squeezing it in hers. Paty shook her head, recalling the day they'd met. "She looked so sad. So alone."

Joss struggled to wrap his mind around Paty's betrayal. The irony that the Slayer Society had assigned Paty to assist in keeping a close watch on Joss due to their inability to fully trust him did not escape him.

"I offered to help her, but she was inconsolable. So I picked her up to carry her to the police station. I couldn't leave her there, Joss. She was just a little girl, all alone in Manhattan. I had to help her." The look in her eyes was almost apologetic. Almost, but not quite. "When I picked her up, she nuzzled into my neck. That's when she bit me. That's when I became bound to her and duty sworn to protect her at any cost."

Paty had not only betrayed the Society, but had also put the people in Santa Carla in immediate danger by allowing his sister to run wild with her appetite unchecked. Furious, he balled his hands into fists, squeezing them into his sides. "You swore to protect . . . Cecile."

Paty offered a curt nod, and no apology or further explanation. "Even from her brother, the Slayer."

Joss had to fight to keep any semblance of calm in his tone. He held her gaze, doing his best to reason with her. In the way that a Slayer was supposed to in a situation like this. "Paty, she's a vampire and she's controlling you."

Paty shook her head. There would be no changing her mind at this moment, no reminding her of the oath that she'd taken to the Slayer Society. Not today.

Maybe not ever. Her eyes glinted with stubbornness. "You don't understand, Joss. You never will."

He understood better than she ever could under the veil of fog that a vampire's power draped over their drudge. It was a veil that enforced absolute control, but Paty couldn't see that just yet. She was lost in the fog, and Joss's stake was the beacon that would lead her back to reality.

"Believe me, I do. She's my sister. No one on Earth could love her more than I do. That's why I can't let her exist like this." His eyes found Cecile once again, but only for a moment. He couldn't look at her for very long without aching to embrace the sister that he'd lost those years ago. But this creature, no matter how similar looking, wasn't Cecile. It couldn't be. It had fangs.

The same way that Vlad had fangs. The same way that Sirus had had fangs. When he'd seen his stake in each of them, it had broken him. He'd liked Vlad. He'd trusted Sirus. What did that say about him as a Slayer? Was he still a Slayer, or something else now. Was he changing? And if so, into what? And was it such a bad thing? He was so confused.

Paty's words came out in a defensive growl. "You won't get past me, Joss. Don't make me kill you. You're too good a friend."

"Did you know that she'd planned on killing me, Paty?"

Paty set her jaw, which Joss could only take to mean yes. It was astounding how drastically a vampire could twist their drudge's mind. More frightening than anything that Joss could imagine. "You don't understand. She'd been ordered to take your life, and then ordered me not to stand in her way. I could only do so much. I warned you to protect your cousin—that's as much as I could do. She's not a monster, Joss. She's just a little girl."

"When she's gone, Paty, you'll realize that what you're doing is wrong." Joss picked up his stake, ready to do what had to be done. "I have to do this . . . for both of you. For all of us."

Paty snarled. "Like hell you do."

Joss couldn't recall seeing Paty withdraw her stake, but before he realized, it was there in her hands, and she was moving toward him in a cat-like stance. Joss gripped his stake tightly and countered her moves. They circled one another with eyes locked, like two animals about to engage.

Paty lunged, striking out at Joss with her stake. He jumped back, holding his arms up in a guarded stance. She moved again, but he dodged it. "Paty, don't do this."

"I have no choice, Joss. She means too much to me." She lunged again, and Joss moved backward, the tip of her stake just barely catching the fabric of his shirt. The look in her eyes said it was ticking her off that a less-experienced Slayer was able to escape her attacks with such easy flair. Finally, her cool control exploded into anger. "Enough of this!"

Paty jumped, tackling Joss and pulling him down to the ground. She gripped his wrist, just as he did hers, preventing any advance of the other's stake. It seemed to Joss that they were at a standstill, wrestling uselessly as Cecile looked on. He wondered briefly if the vampire would join in, come to her drudge's defense, but Cecile never moved. She merely watched, furrowing her brow, and waited for a victor to declare themselves. It was as if she was torn between her mother figure and her brother and couldn't decide who to root for.

Joss broke free, but before he could roll away, Paty caught him in the jaw with a punch that made his entire skull feel like it was going to implode. His jaw tingled as he rolled away from her and scrambled to his feet. There was no way that he was going to get out of this with a bit of reasoning. Paty was going to have to be dealt with, in a language that a Slayer like her could well understand.

Moving as fast as he was able to, Joss threw two quick punches as Paty moved to get to her feet, connecting his right hand to her left eye and then his left hand to the right side of her jaw. Paty scrambled to her feet with a grunt and wiped the blood from her lip with the back of her hand. She looked at the blood and then at Joss. "Well, well, well, looks like you were paying attention during your sessions with Abraham. Just don't forget, he was my teacher, too."

Paty jumped toward him, the bottom of her sneaker making contact with the side of Joss's head, knocking him to the ground. Joss caught himself with his hands. As he rolled and quickly regained his footing, he felt his palms stinging slightly, and knew that he'd scraped them like crazy on the forest floor.

Before he could make a move, Paty lunged in with her stake again, aiming for his heart. Joss shot out his right hand and grabbed her wrist. As quickly as he was able, he used her momentum against her and pulled. As she moved past him, he placed a hard kick in the small of her back, crashing her into a tree. Paty swore as she made contact, but Cecile still didn't move.

Grabbing a handful of Paty's hair, Joss slammed her face into the tree several times. She would never stop. Not until he made her stop.

Her stake tumbled to the forest floor. Once Joss had ceased his assault, Paty crumbled to the ground, her nose split and bleeding profusely. As she slowly got to all fours, she picked up her stake once again.

Joss backed off but kept up a defensive stance. He'd clearly won the fight. There was no need for it to go any further. There was no need for anyone to die here. "We're done now, Paty. It's over."

Cecile moved at last, timidly stepping closer to Paty as she gripped her stake in one hand and used the other on the tree to bring herself to standing. Suddenly, she pushed Cecile out of the way and drew her arm back before launching her stake straight at Joss.

Instinctively, Joss returned fire with his own stake, throwing it at Paty.

Joss's left shoulder lit up with a heat like no other he'd felt before. Paty's stake slammed through his shoulder. All the way through. As Joss fell to the ground, the heat became lightning. Pain. So much pain.

As he fell to the ground, Joss looked to the right and realized how wrong he'd been. Cecile lay on the ground, Joss's stake sticking out of her chest. There was blood all over her pretty dress, but none, he noticed, on her mouth. He'd staked her. He'd murdered his baby sister.

The last thing he heard before the darkness of pain and anguish overtook him was a scream, followed by Paty's sobs.

· 18 ·

VISITING HOURS

Consciousness tugged at Joss, whispering into his ear with the sounds of the world. Sounds of movement, voices, machinery. Joss fought it off as long as he could, not wanting to wake in a world where he had just killed his sister, wanting only to float in the haze of nowhere and nothing and pretend that he wasn't the worst person on the face of the earth.

Henry had been right, after all. He was a monster. A monster of the worst sort. The kind of monster that exhibits no loyalty, no kindness, no love at all. It didn't matter that his action had been a fluke, a terrible accident. What mattered was that he had done it. He had murdered Cecile. And he didn't feel at all justified or relieved that he'd saved his sister from the life of a monster. Not like he thought that he would. Instead, he felt terrible that he'd killed Cecile, in whatever form she'd existed in. He hadn't saved her at all. He'd murdered her. And now nothing would be all right in his life ever again.

To his left he could hear a soft beeping noise and the faint hush of something else, a breezy noise that Joss found strangely comforting. To his right, he heard the faint, filtered sounds of traffic in the distance. As consciousness tugged harder, he realized that he was lying on a bed, a soft pillow supporting his heavy head, his left arm aching slightly at the bend, his left shoulder throbbing with pain. The air smelled uncomfortably medicinal. Hospital. He was in the hospital. Of that, there was no doubt.

As Joss reluctantly peeled his eyes open, he was greeted by the sight of a slender, redheaded nurse checking various numbers on a screen near the head of his bed. When she noticed that he was waking, she smiled broadly. "Well, good morning, Mister McMillan. I was wondering when you'd be joining us."

"How long have I been here?" His throat burned from dryness.

"Oh, just about five hours or so. But the doctor wants you to be kept overnight for observation. Are you in any pain?" As Joss shook his head, she turned his left arm gently to the side and examined his IV. When she was finished, she patted his hand gently. "You're very lucky that your cousin was there when you fell out of that tree, y'know. And luckier still that that fallen branch didn't stab you just a few inches over, or we wouldn't be having this conversation."

A tree. Joss hadn't fallen out of a tree. It must have been a story concocted by Henry. How had he gotten to the hospital? What had happened after he'd lost consciousness in the woods? And why hadn't Paty found his unconscious form and finished him off?

Against his will, two images flashed in his mind. Cecile, lying on her bed, a thin line of blood running from the corner of her mouth to her pink ballerina sheets. Cecile, lying on the forest floor, Joss's stake sticking out of her chest. With a gasp, he blinked the images away and met the nurse's gaze. "Is Henry here? My cousin. Can I see him?"

The nurse smiled and walked out the door. When she returned, it was only long enough to hold the door open for Joss's parents. Joss's mom rushed to his bedside, her cheeks streaked with tears. As she rambled on about how much she loved him and how relieved she was that he was okay and awake now, she brushed his hair back from his forehead, stroking it a little too roughly. Joss looked to his dad for help, but even as his dad pulled his mom away gently, Joss reveled in the attention. Joss's dad reached across the bed and gave Joss's arm a light squeeze. "We thought we'd lost you."

"I'm okay, guys. Really." Looking between them, he was surprised to see the concerned sorrow on their faces. Guilt filled him for not trusting his parents to worry about him, but he couldn't help it.

His mom moved closer, but refrained from man-handling him again. When she met his gaze, Joss was shocked to see lucidity in her eyes. The haze, for the moment, was gone. Her voice, when she spoke, was one of promise. "Come home, Joss. I promise every-thing will be better. Just come home, okay?"

She bent down and hugged him, and after a moment of surprised hesitation, Joss hugged her back, ignoring the pain. Some pains were worth it.

Once they'd parted, Joss said, "Can I see Henry? I want to thank him."

"Of course," His dad said as he ushered his mom to the door. "Of course, son."

Son. Because that's what Joss was. It wasn't a false-hood this time. It wasn't some play they were putting on for family and friends. His dad had meant it.

His parents stepped out into the hall. A moment later, Henry walked through the door and closed it behind him. He moved close to the bed, his eyes full of concern. "Hey."

Joss pressed the button on the side of his bed until he was sitting upright. "Hey."

Henry shifted his eyes to the IV bag before looking directly at Joss. "You okay?"

Joss shrugged. When he did, a hot pain tore through his shoulder. He gritted his teeth and said, "I guess. The nurse said you saw me fall out of a tree."

"Yeah, that's what I've been telling people. I saw everything, Joss. After the whole thing with Kat, I realized you'd disappeared, so I started looking for you. When I found you, I saw you and that woman fighting, but before I could help or anything, she'd staked you." The next words he spoke were but a whisper of shock. "Was . . . was that really Cecile?"

"Yeah. It turns out she didn't die back then after all. She's a vampire. Or . . . she was." The image of Cecile lying dead on the forest floor threatened to resurface in his memories then, but Joss clamped down on his thoughts and did all that he could to keep them at bay.

"I'm so sorry." Henry's eyes glistened, even in the low light of Joss's hospital room.

Joss nodded his gratitude, for Henry's empathy and for bringing him to the hospital, despite the fact that they'd been at odds. For being his brother, the way he'd always been. "What about Kat? Is she okay?"

Upon hearing Kat's name, Henry's jaw tightened

some, the threat of tears drying in his eyes. It was clear to Joss that whatever feelings that Henry had had for Kat had completely evaporated since Joss had seen them last. "She's fine. Being slammed against that building stunned her a bit, but no real harm was done. Apart from a broken wrist, that is."

Henry shrugged casually, but Joss could tell that his encounter with Kat had deeply troubled him. But Henry had a need to appear strong, and Joss respected that. "Anyway, when she recovered, before I ran off after you, I demanded to know why she was trying to kill me and why she hated you so much. She swore you're evil to the core and trying to eradicate vampires everywhere."

Joss sank down some in the hospital bed. He furrowed his brow, wondering how right or wrong Kat might be.

With a heavy sigh, Henry said, "After a while, I just walked away. Because I know there's good in you, Joss. And if Kat can't see that, then good riddance."

Joss could hardly believe what he was hearing. Not only had Henry *not* chosen a seriously cute girl over him, Henry had given him that solid glimmer of hope that he'd been desperately searching for ever since their freshman year—hope that someday their relationship might be repaired. It was all that he'd ever wanted from his cousin. Apart from assuring Henry's safety, of course. "Please be careful who you choose as friends."

Henry nodded. "I will. So long as you do the same."

Joss extended his hand, shaking Henry's in his. "Deal."

Joss started to pull away, but Henry tightened his grip on Joss's hand, meeting his eyes. "We're brothers, Joss. We've always been more like brothers than cousins. Nothing can change that. But we can't really be friends until you open your mind and realize that all of one type of people are not the same. We can't be close again until you learn to let go of your prejudice. I need you to understand that."

Joss did understand that. But he didn't think that Henry had it right, exactly. His thoughts had been shifting, especially this summer, and now Joss wasn't sure how he felt about vampires or Slayers. He didn't know if it was such a terrible thing to view Vlad as his friend, the way that the Slayer Society had taught him. He didn't know if mourning Sirus or looking back fondly on his conversations with Dorian were wrong. He only knew that he did those things, and that when he did, a certain sense of satisfaction had come from them. So maybe he and Henry were closer than he thought to reclaiming their friendship.

With a meaningful look exchanged between them, Henry released his grip and slipped out the door. As he did so, another man stepped inside the room past him, but Henry didn't seem to notice him at all. Joss, however, did.

"It's nice to see you again, my young friend."

Joss instantly recognized the copper hair, the curious smile, the sparkling eyes. He couldn't help but smile a little himself at the sight of his strange, occasional companion. "Dorian . . . what are you doing here?"

A sudden twinge of fear entered him—one that wondered if the moment had come, the moment when he would take Dorian's life. But upon seeing Dorian's smile spread, Joss's panic was set at ease. Not yet, he told himself. Not yet.

"I come bearing a gift for you. A very precious gift. One I suspect you very much need." Ever so slowly, Dorian brought his hand from behind his back, drawing out from behind him a beautiful blue-eyed girl with cascading blond curls. She looked like Cecile. But she couldn't be Cecile. Because Cecile was dead. At her brother's hand.

"Jossie!" The girl squealed and ran across the room, throwing herself into Joss's arms. Joss inhaled her vanilla scent and realized that it was true. This was his sister. But how?

Cradling Cecile to his chest and ignoring the pain radiating from his shoulder, Joss looked over his sister to Dorian. "How? How did she survive?"

"I healed her with my blood. The least that I could do, considering the things that I have done. To you, my boy. To your family." A look of shame crossed his eyes then. One that Joss didn't fully understand. "The healing properties of vampire blood are widely known in Elysia. One can snatch a person back from the brink of death with merely a taste. And taste my blood she did."

Joss almost asked whether Cecile was human or vampire, but stopped himself. It didn't matter. It didn't matter at all. Human. Vampire. These were just words. Cecile was his sister, and that's all that mattered to him.

Cecile had a small voice, as she nuzzled into his chest. "I'm sorry I tried to kill you, Jossie. Em was making me. She told me if I didn't that she'd kill us both. And Mommy and Daddy, too."

He kissed the top of her head, stroking her hair. It was all right. None of it mattered. All that mattered was that Cecile was still alive.

Dorian glanced at her, a look of absolute empathy on his face. His words came out softly, almost as a coo. "None of that is your fault, little one. This entire situation . . . it's all due to my actions. And my time has run regrettably short, considering what will happen over the course of the next year."

Joss was about to ask what Dorian had meant by that when Dorian turned his attention back to Joss and said, "I owe you an apology, my young friend. An apology that I could not give you—not until this moment, though I'm afraid it will not be an easy apology for me to give. I'm not one who normally is prone to regret, you see. But there are two things that I have done in my lifetime which I deeply regret, and this is one of them. And for that, I must apologize."

"For what?"

"It was me, you see," The look in Dorian's eyes was haunted, unlike anything that Joss had ever seen him express before. "That night . . . I was the vampire who took your sister from you those years ago."

Joss's heart hammered inside his chest, despite the calming effects of the pain medication. It was Dorian. When he stretched back his memory to that night, he could see only fog in place of Cecile's attacker's face. But it had been Dorian looming over her, after all.

"I took her." The words shook from Dorian's lips, further disturbing Joss. He hadn't seen such uncertainty or guilt from his strange vampire companion before. Dorian's words came out in near-whispers. "Though I'd been sent to do much worse. Em had instructed me to kill every child in that house, to do what I could to prevent another Slayer from being trained. I tried and began to feed, but before I could take her life, I sensed something . . . a presence . . . *you*, my dear boy."

The vampire in Cecile's room that night had

looked at him. It had touched his forehead, and said kind words. But the moment, the actions had terrified Joss and shook him to the core even these years later. Somehow, Dorian had made Joss forget his face, with only a single touch.

Dorian nodded slowly, agreeing with his silent assessment. "The moment I saw your face, I recognized you to be the boy from my nightmares, my dreams, my wonderful, terrifying visions. To my strangely mixed feeling of horror and glee, I knew that Cecile would be the driving force behind you training to become a Slayer. It was I who turned your sister into a vampire."

Joss clutched Cecile to him, covering her ears instinctively, as if it would protect her from the knowledge of what she was. His eyes burned with furious tears. "How could you, Dorian? How could you?"

"You are familiar with Vladimir Tod, but you are not yet familiar with the prophecy which surrounds him. The prophecy of the Pravus. Even though you have such an important part to play in that prophecy, Joss. As do I."

"In what way?" Joss's throat felt parched and overly warm, like it had been burned by hot liquid.

"I must die at the hands of a Slayer—at your hands, Joss McMillan. In order for my vision to come to pass, you had to be trained. In order for you to develop the drive to train, I had to take Cecile's life. I had no choice. I am a slave to this prophecy, as are all who are involved in it. Entangled in it . . . as it were." Dorian looked troubled, but very much like he understood that he richly deserved Joss's wrath, if that's what Joss decided to give him. "I had a daughter once. Long ago. Cecile reminds me too much of her. Her sweetness, her innocence. I found that I couldn't bring myself to kill your sister, but due to the prophecy, I had no choice but to make you think that I had. So in the end, I took her human life and gifted her with the life of a vampire. You've actually known the entire time, having witnessed my actions. It's been lurking in your subconscious these years, resurfacing again and again in the form of nightmares."

The horrific image of nightmare Cecile's black, tunnel eyes filled Joss's imagination. It was hard to believe that he'd had anything like that stored in his subconscious. The very idea that he'd ever feared his younger sister seemed foreign and strange now as he held her close. At the same time, relief flooded through him that nightmare Cecile wasn't real, after all, and that now the nightmares would surely stop. Relief flooded through him, as did a question in his mind. "How did Sirus know about my nightmares?"

"My young friend, do you honestly think that you are the only person to whom I've paid informative visits to?" A brief, unexpected smile crossed Dorian's lips. "I informed Sirus that a mutual acquaintance of ours was being plagued by nightmares, and that those nightmares were the result of Em's meddling. I thought it important that he understand exactly where your fear was coming from."

Joss nodded. Sirus had understood everything about him—nightmares included, it seemed.

"When I touched your forehead that night, I'd wanted to erase the evening from your mind entirely, but at the last moment, I'd made it so that you would remember your sister, at least—the way I recall my daughter so fondly. You must believe me—I had no idea that my gift would transform into nightmares." Dorian shook his head, his soft words apologetic. Joss believed him, completely.

A thought entered Joss's mind, brief, fleeting, and wonderful. Speaking it aloud felt like letting loose a bubble into the world. It was dangerous, but lovely. It also didn't matter to him, so he wasn't exactly certain why he was asking it in the first place. Maybe he just needed to fill the space between them. Maybe he just needed to know. "Can you make her human again?"

Dorian shook his head slowly. "No. That, I cannot do."

Cecile's shoulders slumped slightly. She was trapped in this form, in this life, no matter what came from today. Joss wondered if she'd been happy in her vampire life so far, but he was afraid of what her response might be. On one hand, he hoped that she had been happy since she was stolen away from him. On the other, he could only imagine how difficult the life of a vampire would be for a young child.

Cecile looked up at him, smiling. "It's okay, Jossie. I like being a vampire. It's nice."

Tears spilled from Joss's eyes. He brushed Cecile's hair back from her face, kissing her brow. He took in her features, silently thanking whatever fate had rescued her that night. He couldn't tear his gaze from her as he spoke to Dorian his greatest concern. "What will become of her, Dorian? She can't come back to my family. My mom and dad . . . they wouldn't know how to handle it. They don't even know that vampires exist. What will happen to Cecile?"

Dorian glanced over his shoulder at the door, which swung open on its own. Paty stepped inside the room and the door closed behind her without anyone touching it. The sight of the bruises on her arms—bruises that Joss had caused—made him avert his eyes, despite the fact that every one of them had been deserved. They had been fighting, after all. Paty had been trying to hurt him. Maybe to kill him.

But that was past. Now he was just happy that Cecile would have a loving, protective mother figure with her for as long as she needed it.

Dorian said, "I've made arrangements for Paty and Cecile to have a happy, fulfilling life. One away from the evil of Em, away from the stubborn ruthlessness of the Slayer Society, on the outskirts of a small village in Romania. I spent my vampire youth there. They will have every need fulfilled and will want for nothing."

It sounded ideal. So why was Joss's heart breaking at the idea of it?

"But there is a price." Dorian whispered, his eyes locked on Joss's. "There is always a price."

Joss could feel his bottom lip quivering slightly. He fought to keep his tone confident. He had to be strong for his sister. "What is it?"

"In order to protect them, you must never seek them out." *Never.* The word echoed through Joss's core. It sounded so . . . final. "Certain vampires and the Society to which you are duty-bound would surely follow you to your sister and Paty and do them harm. They must exist as quietly as possible in order to survive. You must tell the Slayer Society that Paty perished at my hand and that I was solely responsible for the human deaths in Santa Carla. It is the only way."

Joss looked from Dorian to Paty to his baby sister. Cecile smiled a small, sweet smile up at him. It was a smile that had been missing from his life for far too long, and one that he immediately locked inside his memory forever. Her eyes glistened with tears, and

Joss couldn't tell if they were happy tears or sad. He just knew that he was grateful to see them once again. "Jossie? I don't wanna go away. I don't wanna be away from you again. But if I gotta go, I wanna go with Paty. She's like Mommy."

Joss glanced at Paty. Cecile was right to view her in such a way. Paty was so much like their mother before the mourning, before the medication. She was warm, caring, loving. Everything that Cecile needed. Sending her to live with Paty was the only way to protect her, to save her. He placed another kiss on her brow, this one a symbol of his good-bye. He could live in peace, knowing that she was alive and safe. Knowing that by not seeking her out, he could finally save her.

He had to let her go. Because he'd do anything to save her, and sending her away was part of that. He'd do anything. He'd do it all.

For Cecile.

· 19 ·

A LONG KISS GOOD-BYE

"**C**areful. It's still hot." His mom smiled at him as she set the tray over his lap. On it was a steaming bowl of chicken noodle soup, a crisp white cloth napkin, a well-polished spoon, a glass of orange juice, and one of those fancy hazelnut chocolate treats, wrapped in gold-colored foil. Beside the foil-wrapped treat lay two pain pills on a tiny white paper doily. His shoulder still ached, but not nearly as bad as it had. Still, ever since he got home from the hospital three days before, his mom had been insisting that he take it easy in the comfort of his bed. She brought him his meals and seemed more like the way that she'd been before they'd lost Cecile. Smiling, warm, caring, present. Maybe the thought of losing her son had resonated with her, woke her up from the fog. Maybe his near death had saved his family, the way that nothing else had been able to.

"Thanks, Mom." Joss popped the pills into his mouth and chased them with a mouthful of orange juice.

As he swallowed, his mom fluffed up the pillows behind his back. "Need anything else?"

Joss shook his head, wondering how long that light would remain in her eyes. She hadn't been taking as many pills since he'd been home. Her fog seemed to have lifted, but Joss didn't know how long that might last. "No, I'm good for now."

With a pleasant spring in her step, she walked out of his room, leaving the door open a crack. After she'd gone, Joss picked up the remote control and turned on the television. As he flipped through the channels, he thought his only option for entertainment was a pain medication–induced nap, but then he stumbled on an old episode of *The Twilight Zone*. As he watched the evil little boy wish someone into the cornfield, his bedroom window slid open and Kat hopped inside. His heart beat faster upon seeing her, and he couldn't help but wonder how she'd managed to get up to the second story of his house.

"In case you're wondering, I climbed the rose trellis." She held up her hands, as if to show him that she'd come unarmed. "Don't worry. I'm not here to start anything. Dorian told me everything. About Sirus. About you. I'm not mad anymore. I just . . . wanted my dad back, y'know? And then things kinda spiraled out of control. I'd convinced myself that killing Henry would somehow . . . I don't know . . . hurt you like I couldn't seem to hurt you otherwise. After all, a regular human is no match for a Slayer. Y'know?"

Relief flooded through him. Or maybe it was his pain medication kicking in. "I do know. You wanted Sirus back the same way that I wanted Cecile back."

"Only you got Cecile back." She walked across the room and took a seat on the end of his bed, shrugging sadly. "Well . . . kinda."

It had been horrible, saying good-bye to his sister. But Joss comforted himself with knowing that he'd done the right thing, in the end. As he met Kat's eyes, he said, "We've both lost our families due to vampires and Slayers, Kat. We're both humans, trapped in the middle of their conflict."

Kat sighed. "It sucks."

It did. Royally. "Where will you go now? What will you do?"

"My aunt and two cousins have a place in this town called Stokerton. They've asked me to stay with them, so I guess that's where I'll be for a while." Her gaze fell to the tray perched over his lap. She reached out and took his chocolate treat. She unwrapped it and popped it into her mouth, and only then did Joss have a real craving for chocolate.

"It's weird, but . . . I'll miss you." He meant what he was saying. He'd miss Kat. He'd miss her presence in his life. She'd been a strange constant for him.

After she swallowed the mouthful of chocolate, Kat smirked at him. "Don't worry, I'll text you."

They laughed heartily, and Joss barely noticed that Kat had stood and approached the head end of his bed. He did, however, notice when she pressed her lips to his in a kiss.

Her lips were soft and sweet. Her kiss had been un-expected. But the act didn't make him think about any feelings that he might have for Kat. It made him think about Meredith and how very much he missed her.

He thought that maybe he might one day fall deeply in love with Meredith, if given the chance. And maybe, if he was presented with a miracle of sorts, Meredith Brookstone might fall deeply in love with him. It was a pleasant daydream, and one that Kat's kiss had sent him spiraling into heartfirst.

As they parted, ending the kiss, Kat merely smiled at him. He touched his fingertips to his lips and looked at her. "What was that for?"

"I just never did it before. And I wanted to."

The kiss didn't change the way he felt about Kat. They were friends—just friends. But it did give him the sense that Kat thought that she would never see him again. Thinking about it, he felt the same way. This was it. This was good-bye.

She hopped back out the window then—out the window and out of his life, maybe forever. Joss wondered if he'd ever see her again, or if they were just thinking the worst, for no good reason.

It wouldn't be the first time.

· 20 ·

BREAKING THE SEAL

Joss had just scurried across the castle battlement with a giant spiked mace in his left hand and a six-foot-long sword in his right, sweat dripping from his brow, his heart thumping loudly in his ears. Behind him was a scourge of angry orcs and their fearless leader, Henry, closing in. The sky above was black with a million arrows, flying toward Joss. As he reached the end of the battlement, he stretched his arm out, wrapping his fingers around the metal ring on the door. He yanked the door open and hurried inside, slamming it behind him in a triumphant move, blocking Henry and his horde outside, the sound of arrows hitting the door like a thousand fists knocking. He turned around and there it was, placed atop a stone pedestal and glowing, gold sparkles fluttering outward from what would soon be his prize. Joss reached out, his fingers just inches, just moments, from grasping the golden heart of Nicktew in his hands. He was there. He'd won.

Strangely, one of the smaller golden sparkles landed on the back of Joss's hand. As he watched, it grew and morphed until the sparkle wasn't a sparkle anymore at all, but a tiny fairy creature. It perched on his hand, a grin spreading across its youthful face. Then it pointed a tiny, innocent-looking finger at Joss . . .

. . . and his head exploded into a billion pieces.

Game over. With a gory explosion and amazing graphics, Joss had just lost another round of World of Feycraft: The Quest for the Golden Heart of Nicktew.

Henry burst into a fit of laughter, dropping his Xbox 360 controller onto his lap. "You suck *so bad* at this!"

Joss set his controller on the nightstand, sighing in frustration. He'd never beaten Henry at a video game. Not even once. He was beginning to think that it couldn't be done. "Yeah. Well. That's what happens when you're too busy in actual life to kill fairies and orcs in your fictional one."

Though his laughter died down, the grin on his face wasn't going anywhere anytime soon. Henry turned off the console and set his controller on top. "Whatever helps you sleep at night, dude."

It was nice that his dad had allowed Henry to hook the Xbox up in Joss's room, so that Joss had something to do in between reading and resting and waiting for the hole in his shoulder to close. And it was even nicer that he and Henry seemed to be getting along so well. Since he'd been home, things between them had been like the old days, before Slayers and vampires and that whole mess had come between the two cousins. Things had been normal. Fun, even.

"I am so hungry right now. Kicking your butt really builds up an appetite." Henry stood, his grin still present, and headed for the door. "You want me to make you a sandwich or something?"

Recalling the kitchen monstrosities that his cousin had constructed in the past, Joss hesitated to say yes. But the look on Henry's face—so eager to help, so happy to be hanging out with him—made him relent, despite his taste buds' protest. "Sure. Just . . . no Skittles this time, okay?"

Henry snapped his fingers and pointed at Joss on his way out the door. "You got it. One ham and Doritos sandwich, extra pickles, extra mayonnaise, hold the Skittles."

A worried crease briefly formed on Joss's brow then, but it didn't last. "And two Pepsis!"

At least he'd have something to wash the taste out of his mouth.

When the door closed behind Henry, his thoughts immediately shifted to the FedEx envelope in the drawer of his nightstand. His mom had brought it to him this morning, along with a plate full of scrambled eggs and crisp bacon, but Joss hadn't dared to open it just yet. The white envelope had the sender's address as that of his uncle Abraham, but he knew who the letter was really from. It was from the Slayer Society, likely notifying him of his next assignment.

Only Joss wasn't sure if he really wanted to go on that next assignment. So he hadn't yet opened the envelope, trying as hard as he could to delay the inevitable.

Finally, with a moment alone to examine it, Joss pulled open the drawer and withdrew the white envelope. He turned it over in his hands, hesitating briefly before tearing it open. Once it was open, he turned it on its end, dropping its contents into the palm of his other hand. It took him more than a moment to look at what the Society had sent to him. When he looked down, he saw a small, square piece of parchment. It was held closed with a burgundy wax seal which bore the initials S.S. His orders, as he'd expected, had arrived.

He ran a thumb over the seal, his thoughts on everything that had happened this summer. Sirus. Kat.

Cecile. Every moment had felt so big to him, so life-changing. And his life *had* been changed. Forever.

What's more, he felt very much like his mind had been changed as well. About whether or not all vampires were evil. And he wasn't certain that he wanted to interact with his fellow Slayers until he was more confident in his thought process. But the letter, and by extension the Slayer Society, wouldn't wait.

Pinching the wax seal between his hands, he snapped the seal in two. With a deep breath, he unfolded the parchment and began to read.

Slayer,
You are hereby ordered to report immediately to London Headquarters to debrief Society elders on your recent activities and the results of your current assignment in Santa Carla, California, in the United States. All travel arrangements have been made and are enclosed herewith. You should know, in preface to your journey here, that your solo mission in Santa Carla was merely a part of your purification over the last year, as was your assignment in New York. Slayers requiring purification face a unique experience and time line to complete that experience, and your purification is still underway.

You should also be made aware of the following. It is the Society's belief that you have failed to extinguish the vampires Vladimir Tod and Dorian [last name unknown] due to the fact that your loyalties to the Slayer Society have been wavering. Your faith in our protocol and conduct has weakened, allowing impure thoughts about vampires to enter your young and inexperienced mind, effectively poisoning you. It is our duty, as your brothers and sisters in arms, to purify you of those thoughts and eradicate those questions from your mind. When you arrive at Headquarters, the last and most difficult part of your purification will begin. It will not stop until you have seen the error of your ways and all doubts in the Slayer Society's motives have been erased.

The letter wasn't signed. It was simply stamped with the same initials that were on the wax seal. Joss folded it back up, shaking his head, his brow furrowed in a most disturbed way. He had to go, had to tell them that he was considering leaving their ranks. It was the honorable thing to do. He had to say good-bye, no matter what their threats hinted at.

A single image, a single memory tormented his thoughts upon finishing the Society's letter to him. It was a prediction of what was waiting for him in London, of what would happen to him, and he wondered how he would feel about Sirus, Dorian, Vlad, all vampires . . . once the Society had had their fill of purifying him.

The image playing on a loop in his horrified imagination was the haunting memory of his uncle Abraham, picking up a whip.

·21·

BACK TO NORMAL

When Joss reached for one of Henry's suitcases, his shoulder ached, despite the fact that he was using his good arm. His doctor had praised how quickly his healing process had been moving along, not to mention how great he'd been doing in physical therapy. But his shoulder still ached, even after two weeks, and he was still trying to get used to actually using that arm in everyday tasks, so he grabbed the lighter backpack instead.

Helping Henry carry his bags down to the car wasn't something that he was really looking forward to. Once Henry left, things would be different, and they wouldn't be inside the safe, fun bubble of his room. Life would resume, and everything that had been an issue between his cousin and him would likely resurface. The very thought of it made Joss feel a little sad.

Henry cocked a concerned eyebrow at him. "You got it? Cuz I can carry it if it's hurting your shoulder too much."

"Don't worry about it. I've got it." Gritting his teeth, Joss carried the backpack out the door and down the stairs. He only had to rest for a moment before he and Henry lugged the bags out the side door. He thought for a moment, as they moved across the lawn to the awaiting car in the driveway, that the pain was getting too much for him, but with a deep breath he managed to push through and set the bag down beside the car's trunk.

Big Mike grinned from where he was standing by the driver's side door. "Look at you, Jossie Boy! Getting around just fine, considering your little accident."

"Yeah. I'm getting around all right now. It's a good thing Henry was there to save me." He and Henry exchanged a quick, knowing glance before he turned his attention back to his uncle. "Did you have a good trip?"

"A long one. Made longer by the two cackling hens over there." He nodded to the passenger side, where Joss's aunt Matilda was still climbing out of the car.

She shook her head, laughing, and when she

spoke, it was in a berating tone—one that was so familiar between the two of them. "Mike, you just hush now! We hardly talked the whole way. You should consider yourself lucky."

"He's just teasing, Matilda. I'm sure Mike just loves the lyrical sound of our voices." The voice sounded familiar, and when Joss saw her climb out of the car after Matilda, his heart paused for a moment. Not because of who she was, but because of who she was to Vlad.

Nelly smiled at Big Mike, despite the fact that he started making clucking noises and flapping his elbows like wings in jest at the two of them. Joss swallowed hard and darted his eyes around, looking for a way out of this moment. The last time he'd seen Nelly was the night that he'd tried to kill her nephew. Talk about an awkward reunion.

Matilda moved swiftly around the car, lightly smacking the back of Big Mike's head on her way to Joss. She hugged him tightly in greeting. "Joss McMillan, I swear you get taller and better looking every time I see you. I bet the girls are just chasing you all over the place."

Henry leaned closer and spoke to Joss under his breath, a smirk pulling up the left corner of his mouth. "Yeah. Mostly around the woods. With weapons in hand."

Matilda shot Henry a questioning glance. "What are you muttering about, Henry?"

Henry's eyes widened. "Nothin', Mom."

Matilda smiled, giving him a hug, too. "That's right, nothing. Now come tell me about your summer while I help your aunt get some snacks and sandwiches ready for the ride home."

"As times with Joss goes . . ." Henry smiled at his cousin, and Joss saw a glimpse of what their future might be. Friendly. Peaceful. Normal. ". . . it was pretty uneventful."

Joss's mom, Henry, and Matilda made their way back into the house then, leaving Joss's dad, Uncle Mike, Nelly, and Joss alone by the car. Once they'd gone, Big Mike and Joss's dad started talking about gas mileage, which almost bored Joss into an instantaneous coma. Nelly, who apparently also didn't care about whether or not tire inflation affected gas mileage, smiled at Joss and said, "How are you? Matilda told me about your accident."

It was difficult to meet her eyes—especially knowing that the last time he'd done that, hers had been full of tears over his actions—but he managed. "I'm doing all right. My doctor has me doing physical therapy. A lot of stretching, which sucks. But they say I'm getting stronger every day."

An image flashed in his mind. Nelly, putting an

arm around him, comforting him after he'd staked her nephew. Nelly, reaching outside of her own pain to quell his. He'd never forget the way she'd treated him that night. It was a debt that he would never be able to repay.

"That's good to hear." She tilted her head slightly and said, "Vlad said for me to say hello for him."

Shock shot through Joss like ice through his veins. For a moment, he couldn't speak at all, but eventually, the words came. "He . . . he did?"

"No. But that would have been nice, wouldn't it?" She sighed, and then chuckled a bit as Joss visibly relaxed. Then she looked at him with her left eyebrow raised. Her words were hushed, as if she realized how fragile the situation between Joss and Vlad was. If anyone outside of the two boys understood that fragility, he supposed it was Nelly. "Is there anything you'd like for me to pass on to him from you?"

"You can tell him . . ." Joss searched his thoughts for the right words. He wanted to tell Vlad that he'd been having second thoughts about the Slayer Society's rules. He wanted to tell Vlad that he'd been wrong to stake him, and that he hoped that someday, Vlad might find it in his heart forgive him. He wanted to say that he was sorry. But it was too much to say via a third party. Some things had to be said face-to-face, in person, directly to the person that you've hurt. "I guess tell him . . . I said hi."

Nelly nodded, smiling. Once Big Mike and Joss's dad had concluded their gas discussion, Big Mike turned to Joss, gesturing to Henry who was approaching with a big red cooler in his arms, a bag of Skittles clutched between his teeth. Mike asked Joss, "So did you boys work out whatever issues you had between you?"

Joss smiled, glancing over at Henry. "For the most part."

Henry sat the cooler on the ground by the trunk. As he did so, he mumbled around the bag of Skittles in his mouth. "Yeah. Por da mope port."

Mike nodded, eyeing them both. "Good. Because family is important. You boys need to remember that."

"Your uncle Mike is right." Joss's dad looked from Henry to Joss. He then held his son's gaze, and Joss felt comforted by the weight of the words he spoke next. "Family . . . is everything."

Once the cooler was packed neatly inside the car and good-bye hugs were exchanged, Aunt Matilda, Big Mike, Nelly, and Henry piled into the car and drove off, hoping to make it home before the late summer storm was scheduled to hit. They wanted to get out of town to avoid it, if they could. It was hard to imagine a storm coming in, as the sky was a perfect California blue, but Matilda had insisted it would be sweeping across the country any moment, so they left without any further delay.

To Joss's immense surprise, as he watched his uncle back out of the driveway, a hand closed over his uninjured shoulder and gently squeezed. The hand belonged to his father. It was the first act of real affection that he'd shown Joss since the night they'd lost Cecile. Joss glanced over, meeting his dad's gaze with tear-filled eyes. It might have been a small gesture, but it meant more to Joss than anything ever had before.

"You should smile more, son. It looks good on you." His dad's eyes shimmered as well, matching his own. Joss couldn't help but see a glimmer of hope that his family might rise from the ashes like a phoenix. Triumphant over adversity. Renewed. Whole. His dad smiled and gestured back to the house with a nod. "Come on. Let's go make your mother smile, too."

As they walked back to the house, Joss realized that his family was doing something that he hadn't thought they were capable of. They were healing. And this life, his life, might not be perfect, but it was finally on its way back to normal.

Only not back. Forward.